(continued from front flap)

Andrić's story, told by turns with the sweep of a Balkan epic and the savage rhythm of a Bosnian folksong, is bathed in the mystery and color of the nearby Orient. Its pages abound with beautifully etched and diverse characters, detailed with a precision equaled by few writers of our time. There is Zaim, the forger, who amuses the Yard with his interminable stories of misfortune in love and marriage; Haim, the Smyrna Jew, garrulous, complaining, an endless source of fact and rumor about his fellow prisoners; and there is Karadjos, the Yard's chief warden, a ruthless martinet whose attraction to a life of crime in his youth makes him a fierce and unforgiving persecutor of the unfortunates under his rule.

A compassionate tale of despair and obsession, a suspenseful story of colorful people and places, *Devil's Yard* is also a modern parable with many levels of meaning. Its beauty and polished perfection will give it an enduring place in the literature of our time.

IVO ANDRIĆ

DEVIL'S
YARD

Translated by
Kenneth Johnstone

GROVE PRESS, INC.

NEW YORK

Original title: *Prokleta Avlija*

Library of Congress Catalog Card Number: 62-16340

First Printing

Manufactured in the United States of America

It was winter. The snow had drifted all the way to the doors; it had divested all objects of their true form, imposing on them a single color and shape. Even the little graveyard had vanished under the limitless white; only the tallest crosses showed their tips above the snow. Here the traces of a path, trodden into the virgin snow yesterday at Brother Petar's funeral, were still visible. Toward its end the narrow path widened out into a blurred circle, and there the snow had turned reddish like the clay soil beneath, so that the circle looked like a raw wound. Beyond it was all white again, as far as the horizon, where all became obscured in the gray desert of the sky still heavy with snow.

5

All this could be seen from the window of the cell where Brother Petar had lived. Here, the white of the world outside fused with the drowsy half-light within, and the silence harmonized with the soft ticking of the many clocks Brother Petar had repaired that were still working, only a few having yet run down. The quiet was broken only by the muted bickering of two friars in the adjoining cell, who were making an inventory of Brother Petar's belongings.

Old Brother Mijo Josic muttered something unintelligible. It was an echo of his old squabbles with the late Brother Petar who, as "watchmaker, gunsmith, and mechanic of renown," had been a passionate collector of every kind of tool, on which he had spent the monastery's money and which he had guarded jealously from everyone else. Then Mijo scolded young Brother Rastislav for suggesting that the stove be lit so that the list not be compiled in a cold room.

"What a wretched lot you young men are! All you young people are like that, feeling the cold, like harem beauties. You want a warm room! As if we hadn't spent enough on heating this winter!"

Here, probably, the old man realized that his words reflected on the dead man over whom the earth had not yet settled. He fell silent for a moment, but soon started berating the young man again.

"I always say, Rastislav—the hero—is not the name

for you. Raspislav—spendthrift—would be more likely. And it's not a name that'll bring you any luck, my boy. So long as friars called themselves Brother Marko, Brother Mijo, Brother Ivo, those were good times. Now, heaven knows where you get your names from—novels, probably. Brother Rastislavs, Brother Voyislavs, Brother Branimirs. That's how it is these days."

The young friar ignored these gibes and admonitions, which he had heard a hundred times before and would have to hear God knows how many times again. The work went on.

People engaged in computing the estate of a dead man who, only a couple of days ago, was as alive as they are now, have a peculiar look. They represent victorious life, which goes its own way and has its own necessities. But, victors of a pretty poor sort, their only merit consists in their having outlived the dead. They remind one of looters, but looters who are sure to go scot free and who know that the rightful owner can never return and catch them. Not that they are quite that, of course, but somehow they give you that feeling.

"Go on writing," came the old friar's rasping voice. "Write: one pair of large pliers, from Kresevo. One."

And so on, in order, one tool followed another, and at the end of each sentence a dull clank as the object listed was thrown on the heap of things which lay on the late Brother Petar's little oak workbench.

An observer, watching and listening to the two, would have turned his thoughts involuntarily from life to death, to dwell on those who keep count and amass all things, and on those who have lost all things, no longer needing anything because they are no more.

Until three days ago, on that wide bedstead from which the pillow and coverlet had already been stripped, leaving only the bare boards, Brother Petar had lain, or even sat, and told his stories. And now, looking at his grave in the snow, the youth was thinking of Brother Petar's tales. And, for the third or fourth time, he felt very much like saying what a good storyteller Brother Petar had been. But that was not a thing which could now be talked of.

In his last weeks Brother Petar had spoken often and at length about his visit to Istanbul many years ago. Having some urgent and complicated business to transact there, the monastery had sent to the capital Brother Tadija Ostrojic, ex-Treasurer and ex-Guardian ("he was made up of Exes") a slow, dignified man much enamored of his ponderous decorum. He could speak Turkish (which he did with pompous deliberation) but could not read it or write it. For that reason they sent along Brother Petar who was adept at written Turkish.

They were away about a year, spent all the money

they had brought with them and even ran into debt, and accomplished nothing—all on account of the misfortune which befell Brother Petar through no fault of his, but simply through the confusion of the authorities who, in those troubled times, had ceased to distinguish the innocent from the guilty.

This befell them soon after their arrival. The police intercepted a letter addressed to the Austrian internuncio at Istanbul. It gave an exhaustive account of the sorrowful state of the Church in Albania where priests and believers were being persecuted. The bearer of the letter had managed to escape. Since at the time there were no other friars in Istanbul from the western part of the Empire, the Turkish police, following a logic of their own, had arrested Brother Petar, who came from Bosnia, which was quite a way from Albania. Brother Petar had been detained in prison for two months "under investigation" without being given a hearing.

About those two months spent in the Istanbul house of detention, Brother Petar had told more and better stories than about anything else. He had told them fitfully and in snatches, being seriously ill and concerned not to disclose to the listener his physical suffering or his frequent thoughts of his approaching death. These scraps of narrative did not always follow each other in orderly sequence. Often, in continuing a story, he repeated something he had already said, and often he anticipated, jumping a considerable stretch of time ahead. He had talked as one for whom time no longer has much meaning and who therefore does not attach any importance to it or to the regular succession of events in other people's lives. His narrative might break off, go on, repeat itself, leap ahead, turn back, and he might add details after he had concluded it, explain and expand without regard to place or time or the actual irrevocable sequence of events.

It did not matter that such a method of storytelling left gaps and unexplained passages. The young man had not cared to interrupt the tale for explanations or to go back to these gaps and ask questions. It was best to leave the man to tell his story in his own way.

1

That which Levantines and sailors of different na-
tionalities called the *Deposito* was a complete small
township of prisoners and guards. It was better known
as "Devil's Yard"—the name by which it went locally and
especially among those who had ever had any contact
with it. To this place there came—and through it there
passed, day by day—all who were arrested or taken into
custody in this sprawling and populous city, for offenses
committed or upon suspicion of offense; and "offenses"
here were indeed many and diverse, while "suspicion"
was far-ranging and its reach wide and deep. The police
of Istanbul held to the time-honored principle that it
was easier to release a suspect if he were found innocent
after confinement in Devil's Yard than to track a crimi-

nal through the holes and corners of the city. It was in Devil's Yard that the leisurely operation of sorting arrested persons was carried out. Some were examined for trial; others served short sentences here or, if it were too obvious that they were innocent, they were released; a third category was dispatched to exile in remote parts of the Empire. The Yard served, too, as a reservoir from which the police selected false witnesses, "ground-bait" and *agents provocateurs,* as required. And so, while it was continually sifting the motley crowd of its inhabitants, it was always full, the discharged being replaced by fresh arrivals, thus constantly replenishing and emptying itself.

Here were offenders both great and small, from the lad who had lifted a bunch of grapes or a fig from a counter, to swindlers and burglars; the innocent were here, and the falsely accused, the weak-witted and the betrayed, or people brought here by mistake from Istanbul and from all over the Empire. The overwhelming majority came from Istanbul itself, a choice assortment of the worst of the worst who haunted the wharves and markets of the city or the warrens on the outskirts of the town. Housebreakers, pickpockets, professional gamesters; big swindlers and blackmailers; the poor, who stole and cheated only to stay alive; drunkards, cheery fellows who forgot to pay for their drink, or barside pugilists and brawlers; pallid drug addicts who looked to narcotics for what they could not get from life and so took hashish or smoked or ate opium and who drew the line at nothing to get the drug they could not do without; incurably vicious old men, and young men who were already incurably ruined by vice; people with all kinds of warped impulses and habits which they did not bother to conceal—indeed they often paraded them before the world—and who, even when they hid them, could not disguise them, since their every movement announced them.

There were men with many murders to their account and others with records of prison escapes who were therefore already in irons here, even before their trial and conviction. They clanked their chains provocatively, with furious curses on all iron and on the man who first thought of fetters.

To the Yard, again, came all who were sent from the western provinces under sentence of banishment, and here their fate was decided. Either, thanks to connections or patronage in the capital, they were freed and returned home, or they were sent into exile in Asia Minor or Africa. These were the so-called "transients," generally older people, of good standing in their own country, representatives of particular religions or communities who had become involved in conflicts and dissensions at home and had been accused by the authorities or traduced by their opponents as political criminals or rebels. They

brought trunks and bags full of clothes and other possessions which they had difficulty in protecting from the
Istanbul hooligans with whom they had to share their
cells. Worried and withdrawn, they kept to themselves
as much as possible.

Some fifteen one- or two-story buildings, put up and
added to in the course of many years and enclosed by a
high wall, surrounded a long, steeply sloping courtyard
of irregular shape. Only a small space in front of the
building which housed the guards and officers was paved;
the rest was gray, trampled earth where grass could not
even sprout, so many people trod on it from morning to
nightfall. Two or three wretched, anemic trees standing
in the center of the yard, scarred and scraped all over,
lived a martyred existence which bore no relation to the
seasons of the year. By day this expanse of yard, rough
and uneven, looked like a fairground of different races
and nations. By night all this mob was herded into cells,
fifteen, twenty, or thirty men in each. There life continued, confused and noisy. Peaceful nights were rare.

Hardened Istanbul outcasts who did not fear the
guards and paid no heed to any man sang indecent songs
and shouted lewd invitations to their boy friends
in neighboring cells. Invisible bodies wrangled for room
to lie down; victims of thieves cried for help. Some
ground their teeth and moaned in their sleep, others
gasped and gurgled as if they had just had their throats

cut. At such a time a big cell lived by sound alone, like a jungle at night. Sometimes a peculiar drumming note could be heard; sometimes a moan; sometimes two or three long drawn-out phrases of a song, the melancholy and futile expression of some longing of the flesh; sometimes unintelligible voices, low and guttural.

Noise entered, too, from the outer world. At night the ancient double gates which opened and shut with creaks and rumblings let people in and out, individually or in groups. The convicted were led off to serve their sentences or to banishment. And often, after some free-for-all in the port, men were brought in, frothing, tattered, and bloody, still boiling with rage and alcohol and with blows given and received. Then they lunged at each other, bawled threats, and, dodging the armed guards, sought some way to give their adversaries one more clout. Even when they were torn apart and locked up separately, they still took a long time to cool off, and bellowed their threats and curses at each other from cell to cell.

After daybreak things became a little easier for a normal, clean-living man, but only a little. Out of the stifling cells the whole prison population swarmed into the open yard and there, in the sun, deloused itself, bandaged its wounds, or went on with its coarse jokes, its incessant bickering, and its murky settling of old scores. Groups formed, noisy or quiet. Every group had its center, here a ring of gamblers, there a ring of wags; or a man alone singing softly to himself, or another giving a recital of spicy comic songs; or a simpleton baring his life story; or a daft fanatic, the butt of the circle he had drawn around him.

Brother Petar would approach one of the groups and watch and listen apart, thinking "What luck that I'm dressed like a layman and nobody knows who or what I am!"

Here, every morning, outside his own barracks, a small circle formed in the shade around a certain Zaim. An undersized, bent little man of timid aspect, he spoke in a low voice but with passionate intensity and always about himself. His talk ran on the most imposing lines. His stories were always on the same subject and he so magnified and multiplied his adventures that he would have had to have lived a hundred and fifty years to have got through them all.

The sun had barely come out and the conversation was already flowing.

"My God, but you've seen the world, Zaim Aga."

"Yes, indeed; but what good has that done me, now that I'm down and out and everybody treating me like dirt and no one willing to give an honest man a living? Yet I've been here and there all over the place and everywhere I was well off, everyone respecting me and asking me in, and I always behaved properly and treated everyone fair and square."

Then he would stare intently in front of him as if he were reading a memorandum, and resume as if he were just continuing where he had left off.

"At Adapazari I made good and married. A good and clever wife I had, I was greatly respected and my dyer's business was the best in town."

"How come you didn't stay there?"

"How indeed? The devil led me to take another wife. And from that day on everything went wrong. She was satisfactory in the early days, that I will say. But what a temper! It wasn't enough that she quarreled with my first wife and made the place hell, but she went round the town, as they say, with straw in one hand and fire in the other. Wherever she set foot, she made trouble and strife. She'd have set your two eyes wrangling in your head, as the saying is. My first wife's brothers began to lay for me. They set everyone against me. And seeing I was losing my reputation and my customers and that I'd lose my head too if things went on like that, I sold out at a sacrifice and on the quiet, and took the road again."

"Eh, brother, that was a shame," remarked somebody sympathetically.

Zaim sadly shook his head as if he alone could know how great a shame it was.

"Go on, you're chicken-hearted!" remarked a hoarse-voiced man of athletic build. "Why didn't you kick her out, the poisonous bitch, instead of running away, and giving up that good living of yours?"

"Kick her out, kick her out? That wouldn't have been so easy. You've no idea what that woman was like. You couldn't get rid of her. And still, you saw it was wrecking you."

"Well, I'd have kicked her out, even if she'd had the sun between her legs and the moon on her belly," said the athletic gentleman, and walked indignantly away waving his hands. "Women, women! Once the light's out, they're all the same."

The little man went on and told how he went to Trebizond and there married a rich widow.

"She looked after me like the apple of her eye. I spent four years there in the lap of luxury. But as ill luck would have it, my wife fell ill and died and I couldn't bear to stay there any longer, so I sold out again and took to the road. I worked everywhere and everywhere they thought highly of me and liked me because I had a lucky touch. I went to Salonika, and there I married. . . ."

"What, again?"

"I know four trades and I've been married eleven times."

"Aha. Well, what happened then?"

"What happened? Her family let me down, the Jews. If I could lay my hands today on so much as half what they owe me, I would be a rich man. *And* I could easily clear my name of slander and get out of here."

The "slander" was that he had been accused of passing counterfeit money. Worse still, it was not the first time he had been brought up on this charge. It was a kind of disease with him. No sooner had he got off one charge or done his time than he was at it again; and being a clumsy operator, he was immediately caught. And yet, with it all, he never ceased to dream—and lie—about his happy marriages and "his four profitable trades." And now he was in terror of the heavy sentence awaiting him if the case was proved, and he befuddled himself and got carried away by the lies, half-lies, and half-truths which he recited all day long to men with time on their hands, ready for a laugh at his expense. As soon as one circle broke up he slouched off through the Yard like a lost soul to find another. There he kept his glum expression through jokes at which everybody else laughed uproariously. He listened to every story, patiently, unobtrusively, doggedly awaiting his chance; and when it came he jumped in. Somebody mentioned a country, Egypt for example, and Zaim had a story ready made.

"I once had an Egyptian wife. She was older than me and looked after me better than my own mother could have done. Two years we lived in clover. And I was respected by all the townspeople. But then one day ...." And out came another yarn about matrimonial mishaps, into which some interjected sarcasms, while others made off at the start, waving their hands and casting insults back at poor Zaim.

"That's his eighteenth wife."

"See you later. Tell me when he stops."

But the story told by Zaim, that obsessed and incurable forger who dreamed of a peaceful life with the perfect woman, was quickly drowned in a deafening uproar from the adjoining group. There a foul-mouthed quarrel had blown up, of a kind unknown among people outside the Yard.

The very location of the Yard was extraordinary, as if calculated to inflict the greatest possible torment and suffering on the prisoners. Brother Petar often returned to this point when trying to describe the place. From the Yard nothing could be seen of the town or of the harbor or of the deserted arsenal used as a dump on the shore below; only the sky, boundless and merciless in its beauty; in the distance a glimpse of the green Asiatic shore on the other side of the invisible Bosporus, and just the tips of unidentified mosques or giant cypresses beyond the wall. Everything was vague, nameless, alien, so that a stranger constantly had the feeling that he was on some infernal island, away from everything which had hitherto had any meaning in his life and without hope of ever beholding it again. Prisoners from Istanbul

bore the added punishment that they could neither see
nor hear anything of their city: they were in it, yet it was
as if they were a hundred miles away and this illusion
of distance was as painful to them as if it were real. Because of all this, the Yard swiftly and insensibly subdued
and bound a man to itself, so that he began to lose his
identity. He forgot what he was and thought less and
less of what he would become: past and future merged
into a single here-and-now, into the awful, abnormal life
of Devil's Yard.

But when at times the sky clouded over and the
enervating south wind began to blow, bringing the stink
of rotting refuse and city filth from the invisible port,
then life in the cells and the Yard became really intoler-
able. The oppressive stench not only rose from the harbor but struck from every building and every object; it
seemed as if the ground covered by Devil's Yard were
slowly decaying and giving off a reek poisonous to man,
souring every breath and making life detestable. The
wind blustered and enveloped everyone like an invisible mantle of infection. Even peaceful folk became irritable and began to move around in a state of irrational excitement, looking for a quarrel. A burden to themselves,
the prisoners provoked their fellow sufferers or the
guards, who, like them, were on edge and in a temper
over everything. Nerves were painfully taut or they
snapped suddenly like dangerous electric discharges and

ended in senseless actions. Causeless disputes flared up; there were outbreaks of violence uncommon even in the Yard. Some raged like madmen against everybody while others—the older, retiring people—squatted apart by the hour arguing with invisible opponents in inaudible whispers or merely with grimaces and with feeble movements of hand or head. They had a spectral look.

At such times of general excitement a madness like an epidemic or a running flame flared from room to room and from man to man and was conveyed from people to animals and to inanimate objects. The dogs and cats grew restive. Huge rats began weaving to and fro from wall to wall, incessantly and at lightning speed, while people banged the doors or rattled spoons in cans and tins. Things fell out of one's hands of their own accord. At times there was a general lull of exhaustion. But suddenly, as dusk began to fall, such an uproar rose in one or another of the closed cells that the whole Yard shook with the reverberations. Other cells usually joined in with their own pandemonium. It seemed then that everything in the Yard possessed of a voice was shrieking at full blast, in the delirious hope that at some point, at the climax of this din, everything might explode and disintegrate and somehow finish once and for all. At such times the whole of Devil's Yard rattled like a monstrous toy in a giant's hand, and the people in it whirled, gasped,

clawed at each other, and knocked against the walls like
the seeds inside a rattle.

The chief warden and his men well knew the effect
of this foul and treacherous south wind. They avoided
trouble as far as they could—for their own nerves caught
the disease. They watched the gate, they reinforced the
sentries, and they waited for the wind to change. They
were well aware, from experience, that attempts to "re-
store order" would now be perilous and ineffectual, since
no one could enforce orders and no one would obey.
When the healthy north winds prevailed over the south
winds, when the weather brightened a little and the sun
came out and the air cleared, the prisoners scattered
cheerfully in groups about the yard, basked in the sun,
and joked and laughed like convalescents or sailors res-
cued from shipwreck; and everything that had happened
in those two or three days of insanity passed easily into
oblivion. Nobody could recall a thing, even if he wished
to.

The head of this strange and dreadful establishment
was Latif Aga, called Karadjos, which for long had become his true and only name. Under it he was known
not merely within but far beyond the walls of Devil's
Yard. In his looks and in all his traits he was the embodi-
ment of the place.

His father had been a teacher at an army school. A quiet man, fond of books and meditation, he had married when well on in years and had had only one child. The lad was bright and lively and liked his books, and music even more and every sort of game. Up to fourteen he had studied hard and seemed to be following in his father's footsteps; but then his liveliness changed to wildness and his nimble brain took a backward turn. The change even took a physical form. He suddenly grew coarse and abnormally stout. His intelligent brown eyes became shifty, as if floating on oil. He left school and began consorting with singers and conjurers from the cafés, with dice players, boozers, and smokers of opium. He had himself no particular talent for sleight of hand nor any real weakness for dice or drink, but he was attracted by this society and all that went with it, just as he was repelled by all that went with the world of peaceful, ordinary lives, settled habits, and all regularity.

High-spirited and inexperienced, the young man began taking part in the dubious feats of the company he kept and came into conflict with the law. More than once. His father got him out of jail a number of times with the help of his own good name and his acquaintance with people in high office, more particularly the Commissioner of Police with whom he had been on intimate terms since their school days together. "Can it really be that my son is breaking into houses, robbing tradespeople, and abducting girls?" the father asked in despair, and the seasoned old Commissioner replied, quietly but truthfully, "As for stealing, he doesn't in fact steal, nor does he swindle tradesmen, nor does he personally go in for abductions, but wherever such things happen, you may be sure of finding him somewhere in the neighborhood; and if we let him go on in this way, he'll step over the line one day. The thing to do is to find a solution before it is too late." And the Commissioner found a "solution," the only one he considered practical and therefore the best: that he should take into his own service this young man who had gotten into bad ways. And as it turned out, the youth who had run around with gamblers and adventurers became a zealous Istanbul police officer.

It did not happen all at once. He wavered during the first years of trying to find his place, and then he found it where it might least have been expected, working against his former associates. Once his decision was made he showed no mercy to vagrants, drunks, pickpockets, smugglers, and all other frequenters of the Istanbul underworld. He worked with passion, with inexplicable hatred, but also with skill and with inside knowledge such as only he could have acquired. His onetime connections helped him to widen the range of his activities, since small malefactors give away big ones. As personal details were woven together, his intelligence net grew stronger and wider. Exceptional zeal and professional successes brought him after ten years to the post of deputy chief warden of this great "reception bureau." And when the old chief warden died of a heart attack, he was the only man who could replace him. His reign at Devil's Yard began then and had already lasted twenty years.

The former chief warden, a tough and experienced old man, had employed a rigid and classic method of rule. For him the main thing had been that the world of vice and lawlessness should be as clearly defined as possible and that it should be differentiated as effectively as possible from the world of law and order. The individual and his particular offense did not much interest him. Over the course of many years he had come to view the Yard as a sort of isolation hospital, and its inmates as dangerously contagious cases who must be quarantined from the world of the healthy and the respectable by penalties and threats and by physical and moral segregation. Apart from this, they should be left to themselves. Do not let them stray beyond their own circle but also don't interfere with them unnecessarily, since no good can come of such interference.

The new chief warden set to work at once to substitute for this a method totally different in its approach and practice.

Already during his first year, after his father's death, Latif had sold his beautiful old house in the new quarter and had bought a large, derelict property directly above

Devil's Yard. Shrouded by cypresses, it resembled a deserted island or some ancient graveyard. It was separated from the Yard by a wooded ravine with stands of stately trees and a network of fences and high walls. Here, beside abundant running water, amidst old trees, he built a fine house which overlooked the far side of the slope and so was sheltered from the south wind and from the unwholesome smells of the arsenal dumps and the harbor. The house had the great advantage of being at once remote from the Yard and very near it. In its whole outlook, in its peace and cleanliness, it was another world, a thousand miles away; and yet it was next door to the Yard and invisibly linked with it. By using short cuts to which he alone had access, Karadjos was able, at any hour of the day, to step, almost immediately and unobserved, directly from his house into the Yard. Consequently, one could never know exactly when he was there and when he was not, nor where he might suddenly appear from. The chief warden often made use of these opportunities and kept a personal eye both on his prisoners and on the guards. Since he knew practically every one of the imprisoned and their past and their present offenses, he used to say, with fair truth, that he "knew every breath the Yard took." And even if he did not know an individual personally, he recognized the vagabond or criminal spirit in him, and at any instant he might appear before him and *continue* a conversation about his or someone else's crime. In the same way, and even more intimately, he knew all the guards and their peculiarities and inclinations, good and bad, open and disguised.

This at least was what he himself always said, and on this he prided himself. And so he remained all his life in the closest of relations with the world of disorder and crime which he had abandoned forever in his youth, at the same time that he stood above that world and apart from it, separated by his position and by his thick shrubberies and iron fences and walls, impenetrable to any but himself.

From the very beginning Karadjos had "worked from inside," and thanks to this unusual method of operation he was both much worse, more formidable and oppressive, yet in a sense, at times, better and more humane, than earlier chief wardens. It was out of complex and elusive combinations of these contrasts that he built up his extraordinary relationship with the Yard and the humanity that slowly flowed through it like a muddy river. Not even the oldest and slyest guests of Devil's Yard could conceive of any end or limit to these games of Karadjos'. They were unique and personal, full of bold and unexpected shifts and tricks, often violating all the rules of police work and contrary to all social conventions and customs. In his first year he had already acquired his nickname of Karadjos, taken from a grotesque character in the Turkish shadow plays; and the name fitted since the Yard and all its inhabitants and everything that went on there formed the stage and the continuous drama of Karadjos' life.

Stout, hairy and swarthy, he had aged prematurely, at least externally. But one could easily be misled by his appearance. For all his two hundred and forty pounds he could be as nimble and quick as a weasel if need arose, and at such moments his heavy, flabby body developed the strength of a bull. His torpid, almost expressionless face and his usually closed eyes concealed a tireless watchfulness and a diabolically restless and reflective brain. No one had ever seen a smile on that dark, olive-colored face, even when the whole of Karadjos's body was shaking with gross inner laughter. It could stiffen and relax, change and transfigure itself, from a look of profound disgust and dire menace to one of deep understanding and genuine sympathy. The play of the eyes in this face was one of Karadjos' most skillful effects. The left eye was as a rule almost completely closed but between the dropped eyelashes one was conscious of a searching look with a keen cutting edge. The right eye was large and wide open. It had a life of its own and swiveled like a sort of searchlight; it could bulge from its socket to an incredible degree or withdraw into it with equal celerity. It could attack, challenge, or bewilder its victim, or nail him to the spot, or penetrate into the most intimate recesses of his mind and discover his secret hopes or plans. It was from this feature that the whole face, lopsided to the point of deformity, acquired the aspect—now terrible, now comic—of a fantastic mask.

In discussing Karadjos and going over each of his traits, the prisoners dwelt often and in particular on those eyes of his. Some declared that he saw nothing with his left eye; others that it was with his right eye, the protruding one, that he could not see. For twenty years they had never been able to agree on this point, but they all invariably trembled before the glance of either eye and avoided it if they possibly could.

There was nothing of the weighty dignity of the high Ottoman official about Karadjos, in speech or in movement. With each individual case, convict or suspect, he played an individual game, utterly indifferent to appearances and without consideration for the other man or for himself. He always surprised them as if acting on a sudden inspiration. He made his assaults at different hours of the day or night, upon individuals or entire groups.

"Phee, phee, phee, phee-e-e-e."

These syllables were uttered at various pitches and with various intonations, differing each time but always in such a way as to suggest that he was amazed and disgusted at the person in question and at himself and at the business they had in common.

"What's this? Why are you still hanging about here?

Phee! Come now, how did it all happen?"

The conversation always began in this way but one could never tell how it would go on. It might prove to be a long interrogation, inquiring into the most minute details and with drastic threats which were often no more than threats but any of which might at the same time turn into an awful reality. It might be a relentless, demoralizing, and ultimately irresistible "talking to," or merely a heartless teasing without any discernible object or purpose.

If some overwrought and tormented being, longing to shake off Karadjos' pressure at least for a moment, started to plead and swear and with tears, real or feigned, declared his innocence, Karadjos might immediately change his attitude and begin striking himself on the forehead.

"What's that you say? You're not to blame, not guilty? Eh, what's that to me now, my poor fellow? Phee, phee, phee-e-e-e! If only you'd say you're guilty, I might still let you go: there are plenty of guilty men here. They're all guilty. What we need in the place is an innocent man. So I can't let you go. If you hadn't said it yourself, something might still have been done. As it is, now, you'll just have to sit here till I can find some innocent man like yourself somewhere to replace you. So sit down now and shut up!"

And Karadjos, making the round of the Yard escorted by a few guards, would continue with his game, now, just for the sake of the game; he would shout until the whole place echoed and until he was beyond stopping.

"Don't let anyone tell me about anybody: 'He is innocent.' Anything but that. We've no innocent men here. Nobody's here by accident. Once a man has crossed into the Yard he's guilty. He's done some wrong, even if only in his sleep. If it's not that, then his mother's mind was on some wickedness when she carried him. Of course, everyone says he's not guilty, but, in all the years I've been here, I've yet to find a man brought here without cause or without some offense. Whoever comes here is guilty or was scratched by someone who is. Phee-e-e. I've let enough men go free, by order or on my own; but every one of them was guilty. We've no innocents here. But there are thousands of guilty ones who are not here and never will be. If every culprit were to come here, this Yard would stretch from sea to sea. I know people; they're all guilty, only it is not fated that all of them shall eat their bread here."

Little by little this monologue, delivered on the march, would increase in speed and volume until it sounded like a maniac's howling at everybody and everything before him in the Yard, and everything beyond. Yet in his voice, beneath all the gross abuse and the profound loathing, there quivered, barely perceptible, something like a spasm of disappointment and grief that all this should be.

And the "innocent" man would know now that he could sit where he was for weeks to come without Karadjos giving him another look.

It happened that, some weeks later, there came a deputation of reputable relatives of a rich young man who had been arrested in bad company. They came to beg Karadjos to release him since, they said, he was innocent. Karadjos at once changed completely. He appeared suddenly to have recollected something; he became thoughtful, closing both eyes for an instant so that his face lengthened and altered its expression. He leaned politely toward the petitioners, and modulated his voice.

"Did you tell those who arrested him that he was innocent?"

"Oh yes, certainly we told them, but. . . ."

"Eh, that was a mistake. Phee, phee, phee-e-e. That doesn't do. Nowadays they arrest the innocent and let the guilty go. It's the new rule. But, as you have yourself stated before the authorities that he's not guilty, he'll have to remain here."

They gazed in bewilderment at his placid mask, waiting for Karadjos to burst out laughing and turn the affair into a joke. They even began to smile, themselves. But he remained implacably serious, cool and polite, and took his leave. For a while they didnt know what to make of it. They talked about it to their friends, and they complained to higher-ups, who only shrugged their shoulders or waved their hands to intimate that within Karadjos dwelt a devil who spoke through him—and not just one single devil!

On the very next day perhaps, Karadjos, making his round of the Yard, would come across the first of the "innocent" men mentioned and would take up their conversation of three weeks ago. He would step up to him and glare at him as if he were about to swallow him alive.

"Phee! How long do you intend to stink up the place? As if there weren't enough filth without you. Get out of here, do you hear me? Get your rags together and don't let me set eyes on you again—I've told them to skin you like a cat."

At first the man is paralyzed with surprise, then he recovers his strength and fairly shoots out of the Yard, leaving his few possessions behind for the prisoners and guards to fight over.

Karadjos could spend hours at his "game" with a man accused of theft or embezzlement, of rape, assault or murder; he would tease him, scream or whisper; he would play the fool or the cold-blooded hangman or the understanding and sympathetic friend. All these parts he would act in turn, each with conviction and sincerity. Sometimes he would fight with a man, then again he would embrace him, but whether he fought or embraced he would insist: "Confess, devil take you! Confess and save your head. Don't you see that you'll never stand the torture? Confess!"

And when he had succeeded and had extracted a confession and information about accomplices or about the hiding place of the stolen money, he merely rubbed his hands like a man who had at last finished a dirty and unpleasant job, threw off all artifice as no longer needed, and handed the case over to regular channels. But, he didn't forget or entirely desert a man who had confessed; often he would make favorable depositions and help to ease things for him.

This endless odd game was beyond all understanding but for one thing: it seemed in fact that he mistrusted everybody, not just the accused or the witnesses, but even himself; and so he needed a confession as the one relatively fixed point on which to be able to base some semblance of justice and create some sort of order in a world where all are guilty and deserve punishment. And he would work for this confession, he would hunt for it and try to squeeze it from a man with desperate persistence, as if he were fighting for his own life and clearing his own account—which could never be cleared—with vice and crime, disorder and deceit.

In most cases this game appeared purposeless, incomprehensible and undignified in its pretenses and dodges, but in fact it was soberly thought out and it invariably attained its end. There were no repetitions in it and nothing routine; it was always fresh and rose out of the situation itself, so that it confused even the wiliest, most hardened, and most regular clients of Devil's Yard. Sometimes it mystified even those who had worked with Karadjos for years. Tales were told of it all over Istanbul, so inhuman and idiotic did Karadjos' proceedings seem at times, while at others they seemed excessively mild and confounded one with their evidences of sympathy and consideration.

Therefore there was no lack of complaints against Karadjos and the question of his removal was even raised. The ministers discussed it at their councils more than once. But in the end everything stayed just as it was. Everyone knew that Karadjos' rule was wayward and peculiar; but they also knew that it would not be easy to find a man willing to take charge, day and night, of a mob of derelicts, vagabonds, and degenerates of every kind, who could keep a semblance of discipline and order in his Yard. So Karadjos stayed on at his post and ruled Devil's Yard after his own fashion.

Everybody found this the most natural solution—everybody including the inmates of Devil's Yard. Among them Karadjos had always been a staple of conversation, the target of abuse, ridicule, imprecation, and hate, and sometimes of physical assault. To curse Ka-

radjos' daughter on every occasion had become a custom of the Yard. Fascinated, the prisoners watched and
interpreted Karadjos' every step and look, every word;
they trembled before him; they avoided him when and
as they could. Yet these same people would speak of him
with hidden admiration and dwell on his exploits. They
were used to him, and in their own way they felt at ease
with him. They complained about him the way one com-
plains about one's life and curses one's destiny. Their
own damnation had involved them with him. Therefore,
despite their fear and hate, they had grown to be one
with him and it would have been hard for them to imagine life without him. If there had to be a Devil's Yard
and a warden in charge of it, then this man, a man of this
kind, was the best there could be. His methods were un-
orthodox, in some cases inhuman, but there was always
the excitement of surprise, unpleasant or pleasant. This
served, as it were, as a continuous lottery, with chances
for the prisoner. In this way everything, even Karadjos,
became easier to accept and more tolerable, or so at least
it seemed to them, since they all preferred a gamble to a
certainty which could bring them no good. The inhabitants of this metropolis of vice and crime looked on Karadjos as part of their own world; he was their own
"swine," their "bloodsucking louse," their "dog and son
of a bitch," but he was theirs.

Such was Latif Aga, called Karadjos. Or perhaps one should say, such he had been, since he had now grown somewhat old and heavy, had lost something of his former *élan* and seemed to have grown tired of surprising and shocking the Yard with his inventions and tantrums, his sly and devious ways, and his Solomonic judgments. Nowadays he spent more time over there, on the breezy slope of the hill, with its lovely views, and in that commodious house of his, from which he had married off his son and his daughters.

But once in a while the old Karadjos would re-emerge and bring consternation to the Yard as he performed one of his old tricks in the grand manner of ten or fifteen years ago.

With a mixture of admiration and bitterness which, after all these years, still tinged his tone and his words, Brother Petar would describe at length how the "old criminal" had before his very eyes wrung a confession from some Armenians who had been arrested for defalcations at the Mint.

Precious metal had been steadily disappearing from the Mint till the loss reached such a sum that it could not be kept from the Palace. The enraged Sultan threatened the direst penalties on high officials unless the thefts were stopped, the thieves discovered, and the loss to the State reimbursed. Thereupon the terrified authorities arrested first a few of those directly involved at the Mint and then an entire wealthy and numerous Armenian merchant family to whose business offices the trail of the investigation led. Eight adult male members of the family were brought to Devil's Yard. Here these heavy-set and swarthy men arranged their way of life as rich people are able and wont to do everywhere. Whole loads of furniture and rugs were carted in and food was brought them in abundance every day. No one laid a finger on them or questioned them, and just when it looked as if the whole affair would end there, old Karadjos came through with one of his old-time feats.

One morning, when the head of the family, the elderly, stout, and asthmatic Kirkor, was sitting in the Yard on a small bench in a recess of the prison-house wall, the chief warden suddenly appeared and squeezed down beside him on the bench, where there was barely room for one. Without uttering a word he applied his whole bulk to pressing Kirkor more and more tightly against the wall, although even without this Kirkor was scant of breath. When he had Kirkor wedged firmly into the angle of the wall, Karadjos addressed him, without any preliminaries, in quiet but unnerving tones:

"Listen. This is a big case—even the Sultan is taking a hand in it—and it's got to be settled now, otherwise high officials, innocent people, will lose their heads because of you. You're an Armenian, which means that you're shrewd and resourceful, but I'm a match for any three

Armenians and more. Well then, let the *four* of us find the way out of this dangerous tangle. These few thieves who have been arrested count for nothing. They can't make good the loss. They'll pay with their heads. But you're receivers. You've bought God knows how much in stolen goods. You can still save your heads and redeem yourselves. I know you're not guilty, but one of your people is. But until what was stolen is found and returned to the Sultan's coffers you're the guilty one. Come on then, let's get to work. Otherwise, so help me God, tortures will melt the meat off you until there's no more left than there is on a boy of ten."

The old Armenian, squashed against the wall, could not find the breath to utter a word. And Karadjos continued whispering to him. First he mentioned a colossal sum which the family would have to pay the State. At the mention of this amount the merchant's face turned deathly pale and what was almost a death rattle sounded in his throat. But Karadjos merely rammed him harder against the wall.

"That's nothing, nothing. Why it's only about a quarter of your personal estate. Since you gave false valuations of your property, declaring less than a fourth of its worth, the loss is really no more than one sixteenth. Take my advice and pay back: then the matter can be left to die down. If you don't pay back. . . ."

Karadjos then explained his devilish plan to the merchant who gasped and shut his eyes.

Two cases of sickness had appeared in their houses within the last few days. Plague was suspected. It was only necessary to make the announcement and the whole clan, from the youngest to the oldest, would be shut up in the Armenian plague hospital. There at least half of them would really catch the plague and die. In the meanwhile, outsiders or their own servants would loot the untended mansions and shops stripping them of everything in sight or hidden away. Then, things would happen that usually happen to those stricken with the plague and to their houses and possessions.

As he spoke Karadjos kept pressing the nearly fainting Armenian against the wall. He tried to say something, he wheezed and rolled his eyes, begging mutely for a little time, a little breathing-space, a chance to think things over, to have a talk with his people; but Karadjos allowed him neither time nor space, repeating in his ghoulish whisper that the thing had to be settled at that very moment on that very bench.

The other prisoners who, as always, had scurried out of Karadjos' way, fleeing into their cells or into far corners of the Yard, had not seen or heard anything of all this. They had only sensed that in that corner of the wall a heavy reckoning was going on between Old Kirkor and Karadjos. Finally they saw the chief warden stepping into his office while Kirkor, weaving as if in a delirium, staggered toward the quarters where his people were waiting. For a while sounds of enraged arguments were heard from that direction—chiefly impassioned but futile protests from younger members of the family; then suddenly all was quiet. Old Kirkor, supported by his two oldest sons, had gone to the chief warden to discuss the method of payment.

Within the next few days the Armenians were all released, two or three at a time.

For weeks tales circulated through the yard, how Karadjos had extorted a heavy payment out of Kirkor. Details were repeated known only to these two, yet which the prisoners in some way had ferreted out and had elaborated upon with inventions of their own.

Brother Petar often spoke of Karadjos, in a manner that was a mixture of indignation, disgust, and reluctant admiration, and with amazement over his own incomprehensible need to communicate to the listener, so far as words made this possible, an impression of this monster so that his reality could be conceived by others. He was always coming back to him with some ironic comment as if he felt he had not finished with him yet.

He also talked with similar animation and detail about the life of the Yard as a whole and about the interesting, absurd, sad, or slightly mad individuals who stood out in his memories of the inmates. These were closer to him than the robbers, murderers and thugs whom he avoided as far as he could.

Indeed, that side of the yard appeared to have had little interest for him and occupied a minor part in the recollections that Brother Petar communicated, in the last days of his life, to the young man beside him.

2

As always happens in misfortunes, the first days in Devil's Yard were the worst. The nights, in particular, were unbearable. The better to protect himself from disputes, brawls and ugly scenes at night, Brother Petar had chosen a far corner of the roomy cell behind the great broken chimney-stack and there he had settled in with the few belongings he had brought with him. Two tradesmen from Bulgaria were already installed there, "transients" like himself and marked for banishment. They received Brother Petar without many words, but kindly. In any case they were glad to see the spot taken by this peaceable, decently clad man from Bosnia, about whom they neither knew nor asked anything, but whom they assumed to be a "transient" like themselves, and who must suffer as they did, in these confused, sordid and dangerous surroundings.

They were obviously men of substance, and, as far as could be gathered, they had been the victims of disturbance in their country over oppressive taxes and imposts and the inhuman methods used to exact them. Their situation was rather that of hostages; and they never spoke of the charges against them. Though they were worried, no sign of it was to be seen in their faces. Nothing. Everything in and about them reflected dignity and circumspection. They were always belted, shod and fully clothed, as if to ensure that the summons to move on should not catch them unprepared. While the convicts from Istanbul, great and small, regarded Devil's Yard as part of their lives and conducted themselves accordingly, these two could not be said to be living but to be merely enduring existence here until the authorities reached a decision. Their suspended lives waited for them in Bulgaria. There they would live again if they managed to return. Away from their own place and their own people, there was no life for them and they had no use for what there was. All "transients" were like that.

Only one of the two ever left the cell at a time and that rarely and briefly, while the other stayed on the reed matting guarding their belongings. For the most part they sat or lay without speaking or moving. They never looked up without cause. They ate little, and that in such privacy as they could manage, and drank only water, turning away to one side as they did so. They never talked to anyone and they were astonished at, and silently disapproving of, Brother Petar's joining the other prisoners in the Yard and listening to their jokes and stories and even talking to some of them. At all events they requested him not to smoke in the dark, since that attracted unwelcome guests.

After a few days they were joined by a newcomer, who immediately proved to be a desirable neighbor. One more man, a quiet one himself, had been attracted to this haven of orderly, peaceable and reserved "transients."

As he often thought of him later, Brother Petar was never able to recall exactly when he arrived nor how he arrived in search of that little space nor what he had said on that occasion. With intimate acquaintances, we generally forget the details of the first meeting. It is as if we had always known them and as if they had always been with us. What he recalled, as in a confused flashback was, at dusk, seeing bent over him, the silhouette of a tall, stooping, youngish man, with a blanket in one hand and a leather bag in the other. The two Bulgarians exchanged swift sidelong glances, first with each other and then both of them with Brother Petar—an immediate and unmistakable expression of their disapproval, caution and defensive solidarity. A Turk! The newcomer took his place quietly, almost without moving. You could not hear him breathe. And whenever he woke up that night (there was no one here who slept soundly) Brother Petar sensed that the "new one" beside him was also awake.

At daybreak, by the pale radiance of dawn, which in the open air outside must have been glorious, Brother Petar turned his eyes toward the right, where the Turkish newcomer had spent the night. The first thing he saw was a little book bound in yellow leather. A warm sensation as of joy went rippling through his whole body. This was something from the lost world, the human and the real world left far behind by those penned within these walls. It was beautiful, but as shadowy as a dream. He blinked his eyes but the book remained where it was; it actually was—a book. His gaze then traveled farther and he saw that the book was in the lap of a man half sitting, half lying, propped against a small trunk. It was the man of the night before. Beside him was a traveler's bag of light dressed leather; under him a dark-colored, silky coverlet, that looked as warm and soft as a costly fur. His upbringing and the modest life he had led had not prepared Brother Petar for the sight of such luxuries. He had had no occasion to think about and certainly none to attach any value to the appearances of objects. But this he could not help noticing. He had never seen things of daily use so exquisitely worked and of such fine materials; and if he had stayed in Bosnia, and if ill chance had never brought him to this Yard, he would never have known and could never have believed that such things existed.

His eyes moved on. The man's face was a fresh surprise. It was the face of a youth, soft, somewhat puffy, white with an indoors pallor, a face quite different from anything to be expected here, covered with a downy reddish beard of ten days' growth and a drooping, fair mustache. From the centers of two big, unhealthy rings, as dark as bruises, gazed a pair of blue eyes, glistening with moisture drawn by tears and the smoke of the fire. To Brother Petar, who had seen all kinds of sick men in his time, this was familiar. Not these very eyes, but eyes like these, he had seen before. Such eyes belong to people who are frightened or ashamed of something, who have something they want to hide. That is why such a man tries to attract and hold other people's eyes with his own; to rivet their glances so that they may not look further, search and explore his features, or other parts of his body or the clothing upon it. The young man looked unafraid and questioning, but with quiet composure at the friar's open, broad face with its thick black whiskers and large wide-set, peaceful brown eyes.

Conversation began spontaneously. Such conversations are the best. At first a phrase of greeting, then a few general remarks feeling their way and searching for a point of contact. They were enough to let Brother Petar see that the Turk was not as haughty as he might have been. Reserved certainly, but with no touch of snobbery.

In this manner they met and parted several times in the course of the morning. Each time they exchanged a few inconsequential words. Conversations in prison are like that; they start hesitantly, and, lacking fresh fuel, soon peter out into a mistrustful silence in which each of the participants ponders over what he has said and what he has heard.

At lunchtime they lost sight of each other. In the afternoon they resumed their talk. It was established that both read Italian. They even exchanged a few words in that language, though by way of jest. Yet in some way this hedged them off from the world about them and brought them closer to each other. They talked about cities and countries the world over and then of books, but as they had not read the same books the conversation flagged. They told each other their names. The young man was called Djamil. Brother Petar disclosed his own name but not his calling. Apart from this neither of them said a word about himself or about what had brought him here. The whole exchange moved in a closed circle and among the superficialities of life. The young Turk was particularly reserved. In his somber, deep voice and with a gentle nodding of the head he hardly more than assented to what Brother Petar said, and he gave his agreement to everything without reflection. He himself ventured no observation, not even the most commonplace. Often he stopped in the middle of a sentence. His gaze kept wandering off into the distance.

Brother Petar was a livelier talker. He was glad to have found this companion but he also remembered, "I am talking to a sick man." One did not need to know men as well as he knew them to reach that conclusion.

"Yes, yes," the young Turk would say, with a touch of Occidental politeness, but that "yes, yes" acknowledged Brother Petar's idea about him rather than the words Brother Petar had just spoken.

Still, such as they were, these conversations appeared to be agreeable to both prisoners, like unexpected gifts particularly welcome in the Yard where there was so little to hope for. That is why the conversations were constantly renewed, and continued after each interruption.

The two Bulgarian merchants watched them with covert astonishment and with a mistrust still more carefully concealed.

When it began to get dark the young Turk and Brother Petar ate together. Or rather, Brother Petar ate while the young man absent-mindedly chewed the same mouthful over and over again. In his straightforward manner Brother Petar said to him, "Djamil Effendi, don't take offense, but it's no good, not eating." And he went on to explain that a man in trouble needs to eat more and to be stronger and more cheerful than when he is in good circumstances.

"Yes, yes," the young man agreed, but ate no more than before.

The next day their conversations were longer, more animated and more spontaneous. The time passed more agreeably and the evening drew on quicker. With twilight their talk grew slower and sparser. Only Brother Petar spoke. Even that vague "yes, yes" began to fail. The younger man withdrew more and more into himself and made his general assent only by raising and lowering his heavy eyelids, taking no real part in anything.

From the reddish light in the sky and on the wispy tops of the cypresses visible above the high wall it could be seen that the sun was setting somewhere over there on the other side of the invisible city. For a while the whole Yard was filled with the rosy afterglow; but it drained swiftly away as from a tilted square vessel, and was refilled with the shadows of the dusk.

Guards herded the prisoners indoors, but the prisoners, like an unruly flock, broke away to hide in the remoter parts of the Yard. No one felt like leaving what remained of the daylight for the gloomy cells. There were cries and blows.

At that moment a guard came running to the cell in which the friar and Djamil were sitting. He shouted the young man's name. A few steps behind came another guard also shouting and with even greater vigor. In places like these when the higher authorities give positive orders, underlings scurry to carry them out, and show equal zeal, whether it be for good or ill. In this case it happened to be for good. With a solicitude rare here, both guards summoned the young man to proceed at once to other quarters which had been allotted to him. They helped him to collect his things. It was clear that he was going somewhere better.

The young man responded to this unexpected attention as to an order, showing little surprise and asking no question. Before leaving he turned to his companion as if he were about to tell him something important and, for the first time, explicit; but he merely smiled and nodded as if greeting him from a distance.

They parted silently, like old and intimate friends who can understand without words.

That night Brother Petar thought long about the peculiar Turk. Whether or not he was a Turk, he was certainly an unhappy man. At times, when Petar had dozed off, it seemed that the Turk still sat beside him, awake but quiet, with his book and his rare, fine belongings; and at the same time Brother Petar realized that he had gone, that he was not there; and he missed him. When he finally fell asleep—and with him sleep, while it lasted, was deep and dreamless, devoid of any sensa-

tion of self or surroundings—then his neighbor to the
right and all thoughts about him were submerged. But
whenever he woke up during the night he relived a long
past but still poignant feeling from his youth when it
had become his duty to part from his friends and join
and work with indifferent strangers.

As it grew light these night feelings ceased. In the
plain light of day the simple truth remained: his neighbor was not there. He felt the emptiness at his right as
a new discomfort and affliction in this life which was full
of affliction and discomforts, small and great. To his left
were the two merchants, silent as ever, poised for departure.

As soon as it was broad day the empty place was
filled. It was taken by a gaunt man, shambling, unshaven
and neglected, with black curly hair. Making profuse
apologies he explained that he had no wish to be in anybody's way; but he had found it no longer possible to
endure the indecency of the people among whom he had
been lying hitherto and had been forced to seek out a
quieter berth among a more decent sort of people. With
that he lowered his straw bag, laid some threadbare
clothes on top of it and went on talking.

Lengthy and formal introductions were not the custom in the Yard but this fellow's lack of reserve was as-
tonishing. He talked on every subject without hesitation
as if he were among old and trusted friends. He talked

clearly more for his own sake and because he could not help talking, than for the sake of anything he had to say or of the person he spoke to.

The two merchants huddled still closer to each other. But Brother Petar, by his attentiveness to this extraordinary creature—or so it seemed—encouraged his loquacity. Brother Petar thought to himself: "I'm rather like my uncle, the late Brother Rafa, who could listen to anybody and tolerate everybody. He always used to say in jest, 'I could manage to get along without bread; but without conversation, no, brother, that I couldn't.'"

The man started telling his story.

He was a Jew from Smyrna. His swarthy face had a melancholy expression. His nose was long and his eyes were big and their whites were yellow and bloodshot. His whole bearing was depressed and apprehensive. Yet his need to talk overcame his anxieties and his fears. As if he were resuming a conversation of the night before, he talked to Brother Petar in an agitated half-whisper about himself and his sufferings while they were leaving the cell to go into the yard.

"They rob you, then they arrest you and shut you up. Now tell me, please, do we belong with all this scum? I wonder. . . ."

And he enumerated other things at which he wondered, and his wonder had a wide range. He looked about him nervously but did not stop talking. "It's his loose tongue that has landed him here," thought Brother Petar. By now he was listening with only one ear to the tiresome and feverish tales of this strange man, when suddenly he mentioned the name of Djamil Effendi.

"I saw yesterday that he took refuge with you, since he preferred to be with decent people. But now they've given him a room in the so-called White Tower, over there by the gate, where the guards and the clerks sleep and where the better sort of prisoners get private cells and special food. Now I ask you, isn't it awful? For that sort of man, this . . . this. . . ."

Brother Petar gave a start. "You know him—Djamil Effendi, I mean?"

"I? Of course. I don't know you, if you'll excuse me; we just came across each other, that's all. . . . I don't know you, but I can see you're a man of honor and principle and for me that's. . . . No, you I don't know, but him, yes. Very well by sight. Everyone in Smyrna knows him. Everything gets to be known in Smyrna."

Thus, during that first day with Haim, as the man from Smyrna was called, Brother Petar got to know a great deal about the young Turk and his family and what had brought him to this place. Of course, it was only what could be gathered from this Haim's disjointed and incoherent recital, with important details missing and others repeated three times over but all colorful and lively, though not always clear, and cluttered with details. This compulsive talker was also unable to talk of one thing at a time. He would leave off for a few moments and reflect, wrinkling his forehead unhappily as if he were in trouble with himself, as if he understood that it was neither good nor right to be for ever chattering away everywhere to everyone about everything; but his need to talk about other people's lives, especially about the lives of people of higher social position or of those who had met with some exceptional fate, overcame everything else, and he went on.

He was one of those who waste their lives in hopeless battle against the people and the milieu from which they spring. In his passion for narrating and explaining everything, for exposing all the errors and follies of mankind, for denouncing evil and acclaiming the good, he went far beyond what any normal person might ever see or find out. Scenes which had taken place, unwitnessed, between two people, he could recount with an improbable wealth of details and particulars. And he not only described the appearance of the people he was talking about, he entered into their thoughts and wishes, often thoughts and wishes of which they themselves were unaware, but which he disclosed. He spoke from inside them; and he had a real gift for reproducing, by subtle changes in tone and inflection, the speech of the person about whom he was talking, so that now he was the Governor, now a beggar, now a Greek beauty; and by hardly perceptible movements of his body or merely of his facial muscles he could demonstrate a person's gait and bearing, or the motion of animals or even the aspect of an inanimate object.

In this way, Haim spoke often and long about the great and wealthy Jewish, Greek and even Turkish families of Smyrna, dwelling on major events and significant matters. And all his stories ended with a peculiar rattle of exclamations, a sort of woodpecker's tattoo of "Ehs" and "Ahs," signifying roughly "Well, that's the sort they are. And what are my poor life and my case compared with their's and their complicated destinies?"

And where one story finished another began. There was no end to them.

We are all more or less inclined to condemn the garrulous, especially those who talk about matters which do not directly concern them, and we tend to speak of them with contempt as tattlers or boring gossips. But we never stop to think that this human, all too human, and very common failing has its good sides as well. For what would we know of other people's minds and souls, or of other men, what even of ourselves, what would we know of other ways of life and of countries we have never seen and shall never have the chance to see, were it not for people such as these, who feel impelled to tell us in speech or writing what they have seen and heard and what they have thought or experienced as a result? Little, extremely little. Their accounts may be incomplete or colored by personal needs and emotions, they may even be inaccurate; but we have sense and experience of our own, we can judge and compare them with each other, accept or reject them, in part or whole. Consequently a residue of human truth remains to reward those who patiently listen to or read what such people recount.

So Brother Petar ruminated as he listened to Haim's lengthy story of "Djamil Effendi and his Fate"; and this further loosened Haim's tongue and prevailed over his singular suspiciousness. For, in spite of all vivacity and his burning need to talk, Haim suspected everybody, and from time to time lowered his voice to the point of inaudibility and cast furtive glances about him, like a man who has many pursuers and sees traps everywhere.

3

Djamil was a man of "mixed blood," Haim's story began. His father was a Turk, his mother a Greek and a well-known beauty. Smyrna, that city of beautiful Greek women, had never seen such a figure, such carriage, such blue eyes. Her parents married her off in her seventeenth year to a fat Greek millionaire. (Haim pronounced the polysyllabic Greek surname as if it were the name of some famous dynasty.) They had only one child, a daughter. When the little girl was eight years old, the rich Greek suddenly died. His relatives conspired to cheat the young widow and appropriate as much as possible of the estate. She fought back, traveling all the way to Athens to save at least the inheritance there. On her return to Smyrna, her daughter died suddenly. The sea was rough, the boat was slow, and they were still a long way from Smyrna. According to the regulations the child's body was to be cast into the sea. The sailors insisted on this in their superstitious fear that a corpse on board would bring ill luck: that the soul of the departed would draw the vessel to the bottom like lead. Crazed with grief, the mother protested. She insisted that she be allowed to keep the body and bury it when they reached Smyrna; so that at least she would know where her child's body lay. The captain had a great deal of trouble with her. Finding himself in a difficult situation between the mother's grief, which he had not the heart to ignore, and the severity of the regulation, which he dared not infringe, the captain and his mate devised a ruse. They ordered two identical coffins to be made. The girl's body was put into one which the sailors secretly lowered into the sea. The other, weighted appropriately and securely nailed and sealed, the captain delivered to the mother, as if in surrender to her entreaties. When they reached Smyrna, she took away the little casket and buried it in the graveyard.

For some time she mourned for her child and visited her grave every day. But being young and beautiful, she began to forget her grief little by little. But then an unexpected and horrible thing occurred. The wife of the first mate on the boat in which the child had died had been told by her husband how the mother had been deceived by the captain's ruse. This secret she passed on to a confidante who, following some female squabble, in her folly and desire for revenge, told others, and eventually, in some incredible, and incredibly cruel way the story reached the mother's ears. The wretched woman now went out of her mind with grief. She ran to the graveyard and tried to dig out the coffin with her nails. They had to pull her away by force and lock her up to prevent her jumping into the sea after her daughter. It was sheer insanity. It took the woman several years to recover from this second blow, and she never recovered completely.

Many Greeks wooed the beautiful and unhappy widow but she rejected them all; she was embittered against her relations and indeed against all her fellow-countrymen. Several years later, however, to everyone's surprise, she married a Turk. He was much older than she was, wealthy and a man of standing and education, who, in former years, had occupied high posts in the service of the state. This Tahir Pasha lived quietly, in summer on his estate near Smyrna, in winter in his mansion in town. He did not ask his wife to change her religion, but she never showed herself unveiled in the street. The match caused an uproar among the Greeks. But, for all the curses of the Greek ladies and the priests, this marriage between a young Greek woman and the

sixty-year-old Pasha was not only happy but also fruit-
ful. In the first two years they had two children, first a
daughter, then a son. The son was strong and grew
lustily, but the daughter was sickly and died in her fifth
year of an unknown disease, after two days' illness. The
mother, who had never completely recovered from her
first bereavement, now fell into an incurable melancholy.
In the death of this second daughter she looked for, and
found, the hand of higher powers. She felt herself ac-
cursed and unworthy; she got no solace from husband
or son whom she completely neglected. Too dispirited
to take care of herself, she wasted away, and in the second year after the death of her daughter death came as
a release.

The boy, who was called Djamil, was handsome
(he had his mother's beauty in its masculine counterpart),
intelligent and well-developed, the best swimmer in his
circle and also its wrestling champion. But soon he turned
away from the games and diversions of his contempo-
raries, and took more and more to books and learning.
In this he was encouraged by his father who bought
books and hired teachers for him and allowed him to
travel. He even learned Spanish from an old Sephardic
Jew, a Rabbi of Smyrna.

When old Tahir Pasha died, the young man was left
with a good-sized fortune, but alone—he had no close
relations—and without experience. However, he was

protected by the high regard in which Tahir Pasha had
been held. He was offered training to enable him to en-
ter the government service but he refused. Unlike young
men of his age and class he was not a woman chaser. But
the summer after his father's death it so happened that
he caught a passing glimpse of a Greek girl through the
fence of a garden in full bloom. Love struck him like
lightning. The girl was the daughter of a petty Greek
tradesman. The young man determined to take her as
Tahir Pasha had taken his mother. He offered everything
and made no stipulations.

The girl, who had seen him two or three times,
wanted to marry him and found means to let him know
this. But her parents would not hear of giving their
daughter to a Turk, especially to one born of a Greek
mother. The whole Greek community upheld them in
this. It seemed to them as if Tahir Pasha, even though
dead, was once more bent on abducting one of their
women. The girl's father, who, in other respects, was an
insignificant person, a mere counterjumper, puny in
soul and in stature, now comported himself like one who,
in a fit of insanity, has been smitten with greatness, a
hero longing for a martyr's crown. Stretching his hands
as if he were being nailed to the cross he cried aloud before his compatriots: "I am a little man, lacking wealth
and reputation; but I am not small in my faith nor in the
fear of God. I would sooner lose my life and drown my

daughter, my only child, than give her to an unbeliever."
And so on . . . as his daughter's happiness was secondary
to his absurd new role.

These heroics, by the way, did not prove costly to
the little merchant from the steep back street. He was
not given the opportunity to become a martyr. The girl
was forced to marry secretly and without a wedding
feast, to a Greek outside Smyrna, and the place and time
of her departure were kept concealed. The hero was
fearful that Djamil would carry her off. The latter, however, had resigned himself to the rebuff. He had now
come to realize one of the tragic realities of life—the
many things that exist to part lovers, and, in general, to
separate people from each other.

After this Djamil spent two years studying at Istanbul. He returned to Smyrna a changed man, older in
appearance. In Smyrna he found himself a lonely soul.
Everything stood between him and the Greeks; and with
the Turks he had little in common. His one-time companions with whom he had spent his sporting youth were
now strangers to him, as distant as men of a different
generation. He became a recluse, living with his books.
At twenty-four he was a young and wealthy eccentric
who had no idea where his properties lay nor how to
handle and administer them. He traveled along the coast
of Asia Minor; he toured Egypt and the island of Rhodes.
He avoided company where he belonged by name and

social position; and they in turn began to regard him as an outsider: Such friends as he had were men of learning, chosen without regard for their religion, or origin.

Then strange rumors began circulating in Smyrna, vague whisperings that his books had gone to the head of Tahir Pasha's son, that all was not well with him and that things were not as they should be. It was said that, in studying the history of the Turkish Empire, he had "overstudied" and imagined himself possessed by the spirit of a certain unfortunate prince; that he had come to believe himself an ill-fated Sultan.

"Eh? Ah!" Haim broke off his tale for a moment, to elaborate upon the sort of place Smyrna was. Not only had it blackened the name of Haim himself and hounded him into prison here, but it had done as much to such a distinguished and virtuous character as this Djamil Effendi.

"When I say," Haim went on, "that rumors began to circulate in Smyrna, you mustn't, of course, think that this refers to the whole population of the city. What is Smyrna? When you look down from above on those plains beneath Kadife Kale, it looks as if there were no end to it. And it certainly is an enormous place. Many houses and many kinds of people. But if you reckon rightly, of the people who count, it comes to about a hundred families, some fifty Turkish, and Greek families to the same number. Add a few more officials around the governor and the commander of the port, they come to, say one or two thousand souls in all. And that's the lot, because they are the people who matter, and who decide everything. The rest slave to earn a bare living. And these hundred families, even though they may never be friends or visit one another, nevertheless know all about each other. They watch, size up and follow one another from generation to generation."

Both on his father's and his mother's side, Djamil belonged to this minority. The strange fate of his family and his own strange way of life could not fail to attract attention and provoke curosity. "And in Smyrna," said Haim, "people tell tales and then more tales; they spread scandal and exaggerate, just as they do all over the world, only more so."

About Djamil, who, for the last few years, had taken no part in the life of his compeers, the wealthy young aristocrats, there was talk in his absence, and indeed because of that absence. They talked about his historical researches, some with astonishment, others with scorn.

On a terrace where some young bloods were taking their leisure, drinking and smoking with women of the town, somebody mentioned Djamil, his ill-starred love affair and his queer way of life. One of his former acquaintances remarked that Djamil was studying the times of Bajazet the Second, and especially the life of Djem Sultan, and that it was for that purpose that he had traveled to Egypt and Rhodes and was now preparing to go to Italy and France. The girls asked who this Djem Sultan had been and the young man explained that he had been Bajazet's brother and antagonist who had been worsted in the fight for the throne. Escaping to Rhodes, he had given himself up to the ruling Christian Knights. Thereafter, the Christian powers had kept him for years in captivity, exploiting him against the Ottoman Empire and its lawful Sultan Bajazet. After his death in Europe Sultan Bajazet had brought the body of his unfortunate, apostate brother to be buried at Brusa, where his tomb can still be seen.

At that point a young windbag joined the conversation, one of the kind who, by their fabrications and thoughtless talk, often do harm to themselves and more often to others.

"Since his unlucky love affair with the Greek beauty," he said, "Djamil has fallen just as unluckily in love with the history he's studying. He is secretly Djem. He behaves like Djem and regards everything from Djem's point of view In fact his old friends when they worry about him or joke about him call him Djem Sultan."

When a Sultan's name is mentioned, and especially when the allusion is to conflicts within the imperial family, no matter how long ago, it never remains confined to the circle where the talk began. Some bird is certain to be hovering near who takes wing to the Sultan or one of his officers to let it be known that the Sultan's name has been pronounced, and who pronounced it and how. And so it happened that, through the lips of an informer and the ears of a fool, this harmless secret passion of Djamil's became known to the governor of Smyrna, to whom it had a new and dangerous significance.

The governor of the Vilayet, or province, of Smyrna was a harsh and ambitious officer, and a narrow-minded and morbidly suspicious man. Even in his sleep he trembled at the thought that some political irregularity, a conspiracy or something of the kind, might elude him.

(Nevertheless, his zeal and severity in "political and State affairs" did not prevent his accepting bribes from merchants and shipowners. It was on this account that the judge of Smyrna said of him that he was a man with a short memory and long fingers.)

The first thought that came into the governor's head when he heard the report on Djamil—a thought which had never entered the young man's mind—was the fact that the reigning Sultan had a brother whom he had declared to be of unsound mind and whom he kept in confinement. The thing was generally known, although nobody ever spoke of it. This coincidence disturbed the governor. Moreover, just at that time, because of unrest in the European provinces of Turkey, a circular letter had been dispatched from Istanbul to all the governors of provinces, admonishing them to pay greater heed to troublemakers and agitators who were taking it upon themselves to discuss matters of State, even daring to blacken the Sultan's name. The governor of Smyrna, like every incompetent official, felt himself personally arraigned. It seemed clear to him that this admonition could only refer to his particular Vilayet and since there had been no "case" in his Vilayet, it could only refer to the "case" of Djamil.

One night the police surrounded and searched Djamil's house. They carried off all his books and manuscripts and kept him under house arrest, confining him in his family mansion.

When the governor saw the pile of books—and in a variety of foreign tongues at that—and the multitude of notes and manuscripts, he was so horrified and furious that he decided on his own responsibility to jail their owner and send him, with his books and papers, to Istanbul. He could not explain, even to himself why books, particularly foreign books and in such quantities, should arouse such rage and hatred in him. But his rage and hatred did not seek any explanation: they supported each other and grew side by side. The governor was convinced that he had struck in the right quarter.

At the news of the arrest of Tahir Pasha's son some prominent people were filled with consternation, among the ulema, the chief Moslem theologian in Smyrna. And the elderly and respected judge, a scholar himself and a friend of Tahir Pasha's, went in person to the governor to plead Djamil's case. The young man was of blameless character, he said, and his way of life might serve as a model of a virtuous youth and a true Moslem. Through an unhappy love affair he had fallen into a brooding melancholy and he had devoted himself wholly to study. He might perhaps have overdone this, but that was to be regarded rather as an affliction than as a wicked or ill-intentioned act and it deserved forbearance and sympathy rather than condemnation and punishment. The whole affair was obviously a gross misunderstanding. The young man was absorbed in history and learning, and from learning no harm could come. But these arguments could not break through the stupidity and suspicion of the governor.

"I can't bother my head with all that, Effendi. I know nothing about all this history, or whatever it's called. It seems to me it would have been better for him if he had known nothing about it either and hadn't gone poking into what some Sultan had been up to at some time or other, but had given his devotion to the present one."

"But this is research, don't you understand—books!" the judge broke in indignantly. It exasperated him to experience afresh what he had learned to fear as a danger to everybody—the power of people who, because of their very limitations, have an unlimited belief in their own judgments, regarding themselves as infallible.

"Well, there it is, his books are no good. Djem Sultan indeed! A pretender! A bid for the throne! A word is said and once a word is spoken it doesn't stop; it goes on and on and it grows and takes new shapes. It isn't I who am responsible for these words, it's he. Let him answer for them."

"But words are often ascribed to people which have never been said"—the judge ventured again in defense of the young man.

"If they've slandered and misrepresented him, let him prove it and he'll end up in the clear. I don't read books and I'm not going to do another man's thinking for him. Let every man think, on his own responsibility. Why should I go in fear on his account? In my Vilayet every man must watch what he says and does. I know one thing only—law and order."

The judge looked up at him in quick reproach: "This is what we are all concerned to protect."

But the agitated governor was not to be diverted or stopped.

"Yes, law and order. And if any man sticks his head beyond them, I'll cut it off, as sure as I'm the Sultan's officer, even if it were my only son's. I won't allow a hair out of place, let alone the dubious learning of this young Effendi."

"But perhaps the matter might be cleared up here."

"No, Effendi. Regulations are regulations, and the regulations demand this procedure and not the other. He has talked of emperors and imperial affairs; let him answer for it at the Porte. Off to Istanbul with him; let him explain there what he's been studying and writing and what he's told the world about them. Let them rack their brains over it. If he's straight, there's no need for him to worry."

And that was all. The old judge looked at this governor, in front of him. A paltry, puny, feeble creature. You couldn't stuff a nickel's worth of bread into him, and yet he could do so much harm. Always suspicious and harsh, always inclined to take the worse of two possible courses; and when, as now, he was afraid of something, he became merciless. Clearly, further talk was useless; the governor had made up his mind, and would carry out his plan. One would have to look for other ways of helping the young man.

So Djamil was sent to Istanbul under safe but discreet escort. (This was the one concession the governor made to the judge.) And with him went his books and manuscripts, all under seal. As soon as they heard about it, the judge and other friends of Tahir Pasha sent their own man to explain the affair at Istanbul and to help the innocent youth. By the time that man reached Istanbul

Djamil had been sent on to Latif Effendi, to be held in confinement until his case was heard.

Such was Djamil Effendi's history, as known and told by Haim. It has been given here in summary, without Haim's repetitions and comments and without his incessant "Ehs" and "Ahs."

4

Karadjos always shied away from political suspects. He preferred to handle a hundred ordinary criminals, small or great, rather than a single political offender. It gave him goose flesh even to hear of them. He put up with them as "transients," since that could not be helped, but he never wanted to deal with them. He avoided them as if they had the plague and tried to get rid of everything labeled political as quickly as possible. Everything about this prisoner from Smyrna mystified him. He came of a distinguished Turkish family, boxes of books and manuscripts had come with him, and nobody rightly knew whether or not he was mad. (Madmen and everything connected with them filled Karadjos with a superstitious terror and an instinctive repugnance.) He could not, however, refuse him admittance. Djamil was put into one of the common cells where, as we have seen, he found a home for the first two days.

On the second day the man whom the judge had sent from Smyrna arranged, through higher authorities, that Djamil should be properly fed and given a room to himself within the Yard, until such time as he was interrogated and the nature of his case made plain. And this was done.

During the days that followed Brother Petar paced slowly round the great yard as if he were looking for something or waiting for someone. As he did so, he cast his eye along the windows and balconies of the surrounding buildings. From time to time Haim, who had left his berth next to Brother Petar, and the two merchants for another still more secluded, came up to him. He had given "drafts" as his reason for moving, but after two or three days he had admitted to Brother Petar in confidence that he suspected the two merchants of being spies. Brother Petar had laughingly rejected such an idea. At the same time he had taken a closer look at Haim's thin face and had noted in it for the first time that strange and strangely concentrated expression which one sees on the faces of people struggling with delusions and imaginary fears.

Two days later Haim, with lowered head and brushing Brother Petar's ear with his long, pointed nose, whispered a warning about still another spy.

"Stop it, Haim. Don't mention that to anybody."

"It's for your ear alone, you know."

"Now, now, don't say such things to anybody, not even to me. One shouldn't talk of such things." Brother Petar edged away. To be suddenly made Haim's confidant in such a matter left him uneasy.

But this was repeated to the point where Brother Petar got inured to it. He would pat Haim on the shoulder to calm him and try to give the conversation a harmless joking tone.

"Yes, but who? That tall, fair fellow? Can't you see, my poor friend, that he's half dead with fright, that he's not that sort at all! The man's a lamb; you're scaring yourself and suspecting people without cause."

Haim would calm down for an hour or two and then up he would pop again before Brother Petar, asserting that he was the only one whom he could trust, and take up the conversation where it had been left.

"All right, it's not that one whom I wrongly—call it 'wrongly'—thought . . . but it's somebody you'd never even dream of. And who might that be? Could it be he over there, at the gate, looking straight in front of him and pretending not to be interested in anything? Or that one there who looks everybody over so impudently from head to toe? Is it the innocent-looking one, trying to deceive people by looking so stupid? Or perhaps it's none of those, but someone else. No, you can't say of any of them, he's the one; yet you can't be sure that he isn't; any of them might be the one. Any of them."

"Haim, do stop this nonsense, for goodness' sake," said Brother Petar, beginning to lose patience.

"No, no. You, my honored friend, are a good man yourself, so you think everyone's good."

"Well, think good thoughts, brother Haim, and good will come."

"Eh, good! good?" muttered Haim, unconvinced, and walked slowly away, with his head down, his gaze fixed to the ground.

Next day, there he was again, early in the morning, as if to confession. He was never sufficiently relieved of his fears to recover his calm. Then, in his intense way of speaking, always excited over somthing or other, he returned to the injustices done him, the loss he had sustained, and the people and their characters in his home town. Brother Petar, as he always did when the conversation took such a turn, seized the opportunity to put a question to him about Djamil Effendi. On such occasions Haim was never at a loss for an answer. Even about things you would think he had exhausted, he could always talk further, abundantly and at length, supplying new and convincing details. And again Brother Petar listened attentively, scrutinizing Haim's haggard face and high forehead. The skin of his forehead was so stretched and thin that every contour of the skull could be discerned; and the hair which encircled this forehead in kinky wisps was unhealthily frizzled and dry as if singed at the roots by an invisible flame.

When, at the end of his narrative, Haim went away, bent and careworn, Brother Petar followed him with a long, compassionate stare.

Two days had passed and Djamil had not reappeared. Haim who, despite his own personal anxiety, somehow managed to hear or at least guess everything, explained that they must be interrogating the young man. At such times they do not permit the accused to go into the yard in order to prevent him from making contact with anyone. After the interrogation, when the judges would weigh all the testimony, he would again be let out for walks.

Haim the Smyrniot knew and foresaw everything (though not always accurately). In this case his forecast proved correct.

That morning Brother Petar was sitting on a stone, thinking and half-listening to the frantic wrangling and shouting which reached him from both sides and met and jangled in his ears.

To his left was a group of gamblers, who were settling among themselves some long-standing gamester's quarrel. This was, so to speak, their court of appeal. The men were serious and their talk matter-of-fact, crisp and dry.

"You give the fellow back the money," came in a subdued, but commanding voice from a lanky man who was obviously an elder among the gamblers.

"That's what I'll give him!" retorted a squat, muscular fellow with blazing eyes, and with one hand he measures off his other arm from the fist to the elbow.

"Eh, what a man! he's already wounded one fellow and half killed him," voices broke in.

"And why shouldn't I kill him?"

"Eh, you'll do time for it."

"I'll kill him as soon as I get out and I'll work off my time for it without turning in my sleep."

Voices were raised in disapproval, through which that of the tall man could only just be divined, inexorable and full of menace.

"Give the money back, do you hear?"

The shouts which came from the group on the right were still louder and at times they completely drowned those from the left. Here stood the loquacious Zaim and the talkative gentleman of athletic build who was thundering in his husky bass at a new prisoner, a little fellow whom they called Softa. As always, in this group, the talk was about women. Zaim was not yet speaking, probably thinking up some new tale. The athlete was disputing with Softa.

From the little man's jerky shouts one could tell that he was jumping up and down, as small people do as if to impart greater force to what they are saying.

"Armenians, Armenians, those are women, now."

"What about Armenians? What Armenians? You talk to me about Armenian women! Why, you're under age!"

"I'm thirty-one."

"So what? It's not a question of years. You're under age, that's what you are, and you'll still be under age when you're fifty. See what I mean? Too little development, too little brains, too little blood and too little heart. Everything about you is—too little."

"And I suppose you're too much in everything," retorted the little man drily and unfunnily, everyone still laughing at him.

"There you are, you didn't bring that off either. Yes, I'm too much in everything, if you want to know, and that's why I'm no good. Yes, I'm no good either. But you, you. . . ."

Here the husky bass spoke a single short word, which was drowned in general laughter. Then the bass was heard once more, and again on the subject of women. He seemed incapable of talking about anything else.

"An Armenian woman is like a forest fire: she takes a long time to catch but once she blazes up, nobody can put out that fire. They're not women, they're penal servitude. They're a plague that sticks to a man. You're a slave to her and her whole family, and not only to the living but to the dead and the yet unborn. They'll eat you up, most properly and lawfully, oh yes, only with great respect and in accordance with the law of God. (All Armenians are in partnership with God.) An Armenian woman stays unwashed for six days of the week and only washes on holidays. They're hairy up to the eyes and they reek of garlic. But how about Circassians?"

"Those are women now!" said one of the group enthusiastically.

"They?" said the bass disapprovingly, and the word turned in his mouth to a sort of angry sigh. "No, brother, they're not just women, they're a summer's day. A summer's day when you don't know which is lovelier, the earth or the sky above it. But who goes that way must be well shod. Yet again, nothing really helps, even the greatest expert fails. Its not like a bird which is yours once you've caught it. They never stay with a man; they run through your fingers like water; and after you've had one, it's as if you'd had nothing. They've no memory and no heart or mercy. There's no understanding the way of them."

And once again somebody uttered a short, inaudible word which raised a storm of laughter.

Brother Petar whose reveries these clamors were breaking into got up to look for a quieter place. But he

stopped short in surprise. Djamil stood before him, uttering a quiet, embarrassed greeting.

That is what generally happens. Those we long to
see never come at the times when we are thinking of
them or expect them; they appear when our thoughts
are furthest away from them. Then it takes a little time
for our joy at seeing them again to emerge from the
depths into which it had sunk.

They moved away from the shouts and the laughter.

"Well, you see, you see," said Brother Petar, speaking first, and as if in confusion. He repeated these two
words a number of times, until they found a place to sit
down. He got added contentment from controlling his
joy.

Suddenly everything seemed very far off and long
ago, although no more than a few days had passed since
their last meeting. The young man had grown noticeably
thinner as if he had been squeezed dry. The dark circles
framing his eyes were more strongly marked, making his
face seem smaller, and his thin, flickering smile seemed
to get its light from some outside source, which gave it
a distant and uncertain expression. His clothes were
somewhat crumpled, his beard longer and uncombed,
and the man was altogether, but in a different manner,
still more timid and reserved than before.

The friendship between the young Turk from
Smyrna, and the Christian from Bosnia seemed to have

been strengthened by these few days of absence when they had not seen each other; it had developd and matured in the atmosphere of the prison; such a quick and spontaneous relationship could occur only in exceptional conditions of this kind. Even now their conversations amounted to no more than an exchange of observations of things they had seen or read. (Never did either say anything about himself.) Their conversation was unlike anything to be heard or seen around them, and that was its significance. They spent the whole day in this muted talk until the prisoners returned, each to his own cell, interrupted otherwise only when Djamil went to say his midday or afternoon prayers. As before, Brother Petar did most of the talking but the young man's part in the dialogue grew, inperceptibly but steadily, although his voice still sounded like the echo of someone else's firmer and more decisive voice and fell to a whisper after the first few words.

It was in such a voice that on a certain day and at a certain time (once again, Brother Petar could never recall quite when or how) Djamil, hitherto so spare of words, began to tell the story of Djem Sultan. And from that moment until the end he spoke of nothing else.

The start of it was casual, or so it seemed. Quietly and as if he were speaking of some everyday matter, Djamil asked:

"Did you ever, in your reading of history, come

83

across the name of Djem Sultan, the brother of Bajazet the Second?"

"No," replied Brother Petar calmly, but thinking with excitement of Haim's tale and suppressing any sign of his emotion.

"You haven't . . . you haven't?"

The young man was clearly hesitating. Then, after a few prefatory words which he spoke with a forced indifference, he began the story.

5

In a grandiose new setting it was the primordial tale of the two rival brothers. Their contest began with the creation of earth and time and has recurred in every generation and everywhere. One of the rival brothers is older,wiser, stronger, in closer touch with the practical world and better aware of what motivates people, a man who succeeds in everything, who always knows what should and should not be done, what can and cannot be expected of others and of himself. His rival is his polar opposite, a man ill-starred and faltering from his first step, a man whose aspirations reach beyond what is expedient or even possible. In his conflict with his shrewder and more experienced adversary—and a conflict is inevitable—he has lost before the battle has been joined.

The two brothers in this instance found themselves face to face in their struggle on a day in May, 1481, when Sultan Mehmet the Second, called "The Conqueror," died suddenly on a military expedition. Bajazet, the older of the two rival brothers, was then thirty-four years of age; the younger, Djem, had just reached his twenty-fourth year. Bajazet was governor of Amasya with his residence on the Black Sea and, therefore, comparatively close to the capital. Djem was governor of Karaman with his residence at Konya, a long distance overland from Istanbul through mountainous country.

Bajazet was tall and swarthy, with a slight stoop, a composed and taciturn man. Djem was also tall but fair-haired and large of frame, a restless and impetuous man. Though still a youth Djem had gathered around him at his court in Konya a circle of scholars, poets and musicians, and he himself wrote good verse. Moreover he was a fine swimmer, athlete, and huntsman. He was a "hot-head" who observed no limits on his thoughts and pleasures; the days were too short for him and he lengthened them with hours taken from night and sleep. He knew Greek and could read Italian.

Bajazet was the sort about whom little is spoken—cold-blooded but courageous and a leader. Not only his greater age and experience but his own inclinations had given him a better knowledge of his father's huge empire, its laws and decrees, its revenues, and its relations with other powers. He was one of those who, when necessary can concentrate on one goal or task, the most urgent or the most profitable.

In the race for the vacant throne Bajazet was quicker and cleverer. Djem had more partisans both at court and in the army. (It was known that Sultan Mehmet had favored his younger son as his successor.) But Bajazet's supporters kept in closer touch both with him and among themselves, and they worked faster. From his advantageous position on the coast Bajazet was the first to reach Istanbul and take over the government. He at once began to expand his forces to meet his brother who was marching from Karaman.

Djem's army, under Kadik Pasha, got as far as Brusa, (now Bursa) near the sea, and captured that ancient capital of the Ottoman empire, a beautiful, green city on the slopes of a high mountain, but in the plain lay Bajazet's army under Ayas Pasha. Negotiations began. Each brother could make substantial claims to the throne. Bajazet was the elder and more settled and had already been recognized as sovereign in Istanbul. Djem based his claim on other grounds. Bajazet had been born during the reign of their grandfather, Murad the Second, when their father had only been Heir Apparent; furthermore, his mother had been a slave. Djem had been born when Mehmet the Second was already Sultan and his mother had been a Serbian princess. Sultan Mehmet himself, though making no public declaration, had shown a clear preference for his younger son, and that in his heart he had chosen him for the throne. Both brothers were backed by powerful Pashas, some in genuine devotion, others for motives of their own.

As always happens, each brother found enough reassurance in everything about him and enough faith in his own claims and his own strength to support his aspirations and persist in his course.

In these circumstances negotiations could yield no results. Djem demanded the Asian provinces as his portion of the empire; but Bajazet held that the empire was one and indivisible and there could be but one Sultan. He offered to let his brother withdraw with his harem to Jerusalem and live there in peace on a large annual stipend. Djem would not hear of this, and the battle was joined. Bajazet had managed to smuggle in among Djem's counselors one of his own men, Yakub Bey.

Djem was defeated, barely escaping with his life. He fled to Egypt where he was handsomely received by the Egyptian Sultan, to whom this discord between the two brothers was most welcome. Once again, with the Egyptian Sultan's support, Djem tried his fortune; once again he lost. He found himself on the coast of Asia Minor, without an army, and with only a few loyal followers. (His mother and his wife, with their young chil-

dren, had remained in Egypt.) Trapped and knowing
what would befall him if he were caught, he decided to
take refuge on the nearby island of Rhodes, a Crusaders'
fortress, and to seek asylum with its Christian rulers.

Rhodes, which Mehmet the Second had besieged
in vain a few years before, was held by the powerful
Catholic Order of the Knights of St. John of Jerusalem
and constituted a fortified outpost of the Western Christian world. Djem had got to know the Knights in earlier
days, when, as his father's envoy, he had conducted negotiations with them. He sent them a plea for asylum
and almost as soon as they received it they dispatched a
special galley to transport him and his retinue, about
thirty people in all, from the mainland to Rhodes.

The rebel and pretender to the Turkish throne was
received with imperial honors by the Grand Master
of the Order, Pierre D'Aubusson, all the knights and the
entire population. The Grand Master again assured Djem
that he would guarantee his liberty and persuaded him
to choose France as his home until fortune should assist
his return as Sultan to Turkey.

While Djem set out for France with his suite, D'Aubusson set to work to exploit the unfortunate prince for
the benefit of his Order, of Christendom as a whole, and
indeed for his own personal advantage. He made every
use of the hostage he held in his power. Brought to
France, Djem was not set free. Contrary to the pledge

given him, he was kept in confinement in fortresses belonging to the Order of the Knights of Jerusalem.

A whirlpool of intrigue and conspiracy formed round "the Sultan's brother" in which all the European powers of that time took part, including the Pope and, of course, the Sultan as well. Both Matthias Corvinus, King of Hungary, and Pope Innocent VIII sought to have Djem handed over to them in order to use him in their designs against Turkey. But the wily Pierre D'Aubusson held on to his valuable prey, using his possession of Djem to blackmail everyone with an interest in him—Bajazet, the Sultan of Egypt, and the Pope. Bajazet paid him huge sums, ostensibly for Djem's maintenance but actually to keep him captive and make it worth D'Aubusson's while *not* to hand Djem over to any of the others. The Pope promised D'Aubusson the rank of Cardinal if he would deliver Djem to him. The Sultan of Egypt paid D'Aubusson considerable amounts. Even Djem's unhappy mother, who was living in Egypt and never ceased to work for her son's release, sent D'Aubusson money for Djem, which remained in the hands of the Grand Master.

These intrigues over "the Sultan's brother," all playing into D'Aubusson's clever hands, lasted eight years, with Djem transferred from one French fortress to another, always under a strong guard of Knights of Jerusalem. Little by little they stripped Djem of his retinue, till he was left with no more than four or five loyal followers. All his attempts to escape from the hands of the perjured Knights of Jerusalem were futile. On his part, Sultan Bajazet did all he could to shake off the pressure exerted on him by the whole of Christendom through his wretched brother who had become its tool. He received news of his brother through the Venetians, the Ragusans and the King of Naples; he kept continuously in touch with Pierre D'Aubusson to whom he made concessions of every kind. Their interests, in a certain sense, were identical. It was to D'Aubusson's advantage to keep Djem in his power and use him to blackmail almost all the great powers; for Bajazet it was equally important that his rival brother be kept securely imprisoned and not at the head of an army moving against Turkey.

In 1488, the eighth year of Djem's "sanctuary" in France, the diplomatic contest for his person reached its climax. Ambassadors arrived from all sides, all having as their prime objective the person of Djem. Bajazet's envoy, a Christian Greek named Antonio Reriko, supported by the envoy of the King of Naples, offered large bribes to the King of France and his courtiers, both openly and in secret; and, in addition, sovereignty over Jerusalem after Bajazet, in a projected campaign against the Sultan of Egypt, had conquered that city; he distributed lavish gifts to the greedy gentlemen and ladies of the French court. Simultaneously, envoys of the Hungarian King, Matthias Corvinus, urged that the Sultan's brother be entrusted to him to improve his prospects in his wars with Bajazet. But the most pressing delegation came from Pope Innocent the Eighth who, although old and ill, had not given up his design of rousing the rulers of Christendom to a crusade against Turkey. For this purpose custody of the Sultan's rebel brother would be a powerful weapon.

But the Grand Master of Rhodes was pursuing his own plans. He persuaded the French King to let him hand over Djem to the Pope. In February, 1489, the Knights embarked Djem, with a small following, on one of their galleys at Toulon, and after a long and difficult voyage they reached Civitavecchia where an imposing delegation from the Pope awaited them. Under an impressive escort Djem entered Rome to be met by the Cardinals and by the whole Papal Court together with diplomatic representatives from many courts. Both he and his suite were in picturesque Oriental dress and well mounted. The following day the Pope received the long coveted Turkish prince most affably in public audience. Djem refused to follow the others in obeisance to the Pope but embraced him as an equal, as one sovereign would greet another.

Pierre D'Aubusson was made cardinal and in addition to this new status his Order was granted further privileges and honors.

A few days later the Pope received Djem in private audience. On this occasion they talked more openly. Djem complained of the deception of the Knights of Rhodes who had treated him as a prisoner. He begged the Pope to let him be reunited with his mother and his family in Egypt. Djem spoke with such emotion that tears came to the Pope's eyes. He comforted Djem with fine words and these were all the comfort he got from the Pope.

The diplomatic game around Djem was resumed with even livelier moves. The Pope redoubled his efforts to organize a league of Christian rulers against Turkey. In this crusade Djem was to play an important part, and the Vatican became his golden cage. Matthias Corvinus demanded Djem for his campaign against the Turks. So did the Egyptian Sultan who offered a ransom of six hundred thousand ducats, to which Djem's mother added sixty thousand more.

In 1490 Matthias Corvinus died. This was a heavy blow to the idea of a crusade against Bajazet.

Upon hearing that Djem had come into the hands of the Pope, Bajazet sent a special envoy to Rome. The Pope received him in audience and learned of the Turkish aspects of D'Aubusson's intrigues and of the money he had received from Bajazet. The Turkish envoy, for Bajazet, asked the Pope to hold Djem on the same terms as those on which the Knights of Rhodes had held him, namely the grant of certain political concessions and forty thousand ducats a year. Before paying down a hundred and twenty thousand ducats, to cover a period of three years, the envoy was instructed to see Djem personally to ascertain that he was actually in Rome and alive. Djem consented to receive the envoy, but only as Sultan, with all due ceremonial. He sat crosslegged on a special throne, surrounded by his retainers. Next to him sat a cardinal. Bajazet's envoy prostrated himself before Djem Sultan and handed over the letter and the gifts sent by his brother. The letter was read to Djem. Without deigning to look at them, Djem gave the gifts to his retainers, to divide among themselves.

Innocent VIII went on with his plans for a crusade against Turkey, and Bajazet with his designs against Hungary and Venice. In these schemes the person of Djem played a great part. The Sultan sent the Pope "the lance with which Christ was pierced on the Cross," and other coveted relics, asking of him only one thing—to keep Djem in confinement and not hand him over to anyone else. And the Pope warned Bajazet not to attack Christian territories; otherwise he would make use of Djem and place him at the head of a formidable expedition against Turkey.

At that point Pope Innocent VIII died. During the balloting for the new Pope, Djem was shut up for greater security in the Castel Sant'Angelo. The newly elected

Pope was the former Cardinal Rodrigo Borgia, who assumed the Pontificate under the name of Alexander VI.

It looked as if better times were at hand for the imperial Turkish prisoner. He made friends with the Pope's sons, enjoyed greater freedom of movement, took part in ceremonies. In chronicles and correspondence and his portraits, Djem, a man in his thirties, sounds and looks like a man over forty. Stout and sallow, with his left eyelid closed, he had the look of "a marksman taking aim." Moody and excitable, he was merciless toward his staff and prone to excesses, particularly in drink, to which he resorted for sleep and forgetfulness.

In the meanwhile new dissensions divided the Christian rulers of the West. The young King of France, Charles VIII, invaded Italy to occupy the kingdom of Naples, on the pretext of using it as the base from which he would lead a crusade against Turkey. The Pope did all he could to hinder his entry into Italy. Alexander VI went so far as to negotiate with Bajazet for help against the French King. Bajazet sent him the agreed sum of forty thousand Venetian ducats for Djem's yearly maintenance and in a secret personal letter offered him three hundred thousand ducats for delivery of Djem's dead body. The Pope's adversaries in Italy got hold of the correspondence and published it.

Charles VIII drove deep into Italy whose cities fell to him in rapid succession, and on the last day of 1494 he entered Rome. The Pope had no choice but to come to terms with the young conqueror with the least possible discredit and loss. One of Charles's demands was that the Pope hand over to him "the Sultan's brother," whom he intended to use in his campaign against Bajazet. They agreed that Charles should take Djem with him on his expedition against Naples and subsequently against Turkey. But the Pope exacted guarantees from the French King for the return of this valuable prisoner after the war was over. The Pope also stipulated that the forty thousand ducats a year from the Sultan should continue to be paid to him.

In solemn audience and before numerous witnesses the Pope handed over to the French King Djem and his few remaining followers. When the Pope communicated his decision to Djem, the latter declared that as a prisoner it made no difference to him who was his jailer, the Pope or the French King.

The Pope did his best to reassure and cheer him with fair words, and Charles VIII accorded him the courtesies due to a sovereign.

In his campaign against the King of Naples, Charles VIII took along Djem and his retainers and the Pope's son, Caesar, Cardinal of Valencia, as hostage. On the way the crafty Caesar escaped and Djem fell ill. He did not recover and at Capua, before they reached Naples, Djem died.

He had enjoined his followers, who had been with him through all the years of his captivity, to find some means to bring his body to Turkey, to prevent unbelievers from continuing to exploit him after he was dead. He had dictated a letter to his brother Bajazet begging him to allow his family to return to Istanbul and to be merciful toward those who had been his faithful companions during his long captivity.

Charles VIII ordered Djem's body to be embalmed and placed in a leaden coffin.

Immediately the rumor spread that the Pope had poisoned Djem then or just before he had handed him over to the French King. The Venetian Senate hastened to inform Sultan Bajazet of Djem's death, seeking to be the first to bring the good news to that powerful ruler.

Charles VIII failed in his designs on Naples and returned to France, where he died soon after. Djem's body remained in the possession of the King of Naples and a long correspondence ensued over the corpse. The King of Naples had the advantage.

Using the corpse to blackmail Bajazet, the King of Naples concluded a favorable agreement with the Sultan, and at last, in September, 1499, Djem's body was delivered to Bajazet, who had it interred with appropriate solemnities in a sepulcher at Brusa where the rulers of Turkey lie buried.

6

These are only the bare bones of Djamil's story, baldly and briefly told. What Brother Petar heard from his new friend was elaborated upon in other versions, in a livelier manner and in quite a different key. It all led up to the same conclusion: there are two worlds between which there is not and cannot be any real contact or possibility of understanding, two terrible worlds condemned to unending warfare in a thousand forms. Between them stands a man who, in his own way, is at war with both, an emperor's son, an emperor's brother and himself an emperor according to his own deepest conviction and feeling, and at the same time the most unfortunate of men. First betrayed and defeated, then cheated and deprived of liberty, lonely, torn from family and friends, placed in a tragic dilemma, exposed in full view of the world as in a pillory, but proudly determined to sustain his dignity, to remain himself, never to abandon what he held to be his just aims: to yield neither to his implacable brother nor to the unbelievers who held him in their power, deceived him, used him in their diplomatic blackmail, and sold him over and over again.

As Brother Petar followed all the turns in Djem Sultan's extraordinary life, he heard the names of exotic cities and almost legendary men—emperors, kings, Popes, princes and cardinals, names which he had never heard in his life before, and which were too strange for him to remember or repeat. Often, in the course of the narrative, he lost the thread of the young man's story and could not make out who was related to whom or who was cheating, buying or selling whom. At times, lost in his own troubled thoughts he could no longer follow the convolutions of the story, though even then he pretended to be listening, anxious not to rebuff the man to whom it clearly meant so much to tell the story to its end and in all its detail.

Certain things in Djem's story were quite incomprehensible to Brother Petar, such as Djem's verses on destiny, on wine and drunkenness, on the beauty of boys and girls. Djamil recited these by heart and as if they were his own compositions. There were, too, words and thoughts which bewildered and upset him, such as Djem's harsh judgments on Popes and other dignitaries of the Church. But Brother Petar felt this was neither the place nor the moment to sort out all that and offer to set it straight, especially since so much of it was not clear or understandable to him. One must let a man have his say to the end. Here, as always and everywhere, people had come to him freely, had quickly formed an attachment to him and had found it easy to trust him; and he had taken this as a natural and reasonable thing and had tried only to listen attentively to what they had to say. And so it was in this case too.

This tale of the young man from Smyrna ranged far afield and took a long time to unfold. For hours at a stretch he forgot himself completely in his recital of the fate of Djem Sultan, as if it were urgent to report all the facts as quickly as possible, this very minute, tomorrow it might be too late. Sometimes he spoke in Turkish, sometimes in Italian, and in his haste he forgot to translate the French and Spanish quotations which he recited by heart.

Their conversations began early, in the shade of the eaves. As the shade shortened they moved on to other retired corners of the spacious yard to take refuge both from the blaze of the sun and the clamor of the gaming or quarreling of other prisoners.

Brother Petar noticed that Haim never came near

him during these conversations but only when he found him alone. But it sometimes happened that some other prisoner would approach, casually as it were, and would try to catch in passing something of the young man's whispered words. Then Djamil would suddenly fall silent, and like a sleepwalker awakened from his dangerous trance, he would relapse into apathetic taciturnity, broken by a mechanical, empty "yes, yes?"; and if the man lingered he would coldly and abruptly take his leave muttering a few meaningless words.

Next day he would reappear but in the same disturbed mood, and with signs of hesitations and of resolutions taken during the night; and for a time he remained aloof and withdrawn, and his remote smile seemed to erase everything as did his exchange of commonplaces. But that did not last long. In the course of conversation his mood, unnoticed either by himself or by Brother Petar, would change imperceptibly. Without awareness of how or whence or why, he would re-enter the spell of his obsession and talk to Brother Petar of Djem and his fate quietly and intently, like a man at confession.

By the third day the history as a sequential narrative had been told to its sad and solemn conclusion, and Brother Petar could almost see the gleaming stately tomb at Brusa, its white walls inscribed with the finest verses of the Koran, formalized by the artist's incised script into the shapes of marvelous flowers and crystals.

But then began the narration of individual episodes in full detail. Djamil now went at length into Djem's times of happiness and sadness, his encounters and quarrels, his loves, hates and friendships, his attempts to escape from his Christian captors, his hopes and despairs, and his anxious speculations during sleepless nights; his confused dreams when he dozed by day, his haughty retorts to high personages in France and Italy, his embittered soliloquies in solitude and confinement—all were told in a voice that was not Djamil's but some other man's.

Without preface, with no perceptible immediate relevance, and observing no sequence of time, the young man would start with an episode from the middle or the end of Djem's imprisonment. He spoke in a low voice, with his eyes on the ground, oblivious of whether his companion was listening or could follow him.

Brother Petar could not precisely recall when this disorderly, incessant narrative began. Nor did he fully grasp what was happening, at the grim moment when it occurred, when Djamil, as narrator changed from the third to the first person, and spoke of that other man's fate as his own, and as in a personal confession, an autobiography.

("I"—a weighty word, which fixes our position, for those to whom it is uttered; fixes it finally and often beyond or behind our knowledge of ourselves, ignoring our own will and exceeding our strength. An omnipotent word which, once pronounced, binds us forever and identifies us with all we have thought or said, things with which we never dreamed of identifying ourselves but to which we have, in fact, already long been joined.)

With growing bewilderment, concern and pity and with an anxiety he could scarcely hide, Brother Petar listened to the story. In the evening, when he parted from Djamil and brooded over him and his condition (and it was impossible not to dwell on it), he would reproach himself for not being firm with Djamil and halting him on this path of misfortune, for not doing something to shake him out of his delusion. And yet, when they met the following morning and the young man resumed his morbid imaginings, Brother Petar would listen again, almost visibly shuddering but in his deep sympathy unable to interrupt him and recall him to reality. And whenever, remembering his resolution of the night before, to do what he regarded as his duty to the young man, he tried to steer the conversation to some other theme; or, by an incidental remark to differentiate the Djamil who was speaking from the dead Djem Sultan, he was irresolute and unconvincing. He could not bear the distress it might inflict. And thus his native directness and simple-heartedness, which at other times enabled him to say anything to anybody, were drugged and overcome by the young man's obsessed narrative. And Brother Petar always ended by listening without response, without approval, but also without vocal protest, to the young man's impassioned whispering. What was not, could not and should not be proved stronger than what was and what clearly remained; the only possible and tangible reality. That evening, Brother Petar would again reproach himself for having given way once more to this irresistible wave of insanity, and for not having made a greater effort to bring the young man back on the path of reason. At such moments he felt like an accomplice in the young man's delusions and resolved to hold off no longer and, at any costs, take the first convenient moment, the next day, to do what had to be done.

This went on for five or six days. The ordeal began every morning at about the same time, like an established ritual, and lasted, with two or three brief breaks, until early evening. The tale of Djem Sultan, his sufferings and his adventures, seemed inexhaustible. But one morning Djamil did not appear. Brother Petar looked for him and waited and walked uneasily through every quarter of the yard. Twice that day Haim came up to him to renew his complaints of injustices at Smyrna and his fears of spies and traps in Devil's Yard. Brother Petar was too distracted to take in what Haim was saying; his thoughts were fixed on the absent Djamil.

He seemed to see and hear Djamil as he had seen and heard him just before their parting last night, declaiming, as though he were reading aloud.

"Standing erect in his glittering ceremonial dress on the deck of the ship which was berthing at Civitavecchia, and surveying the multicolored throng of the Papal army and church dignitaries ranged in diplomatic order, Djem thought keenly and clearly, as we think only at times when we have left one dwelling-place and have not yet reached another. He thought impassively of his misfortune, surveying it clearly and dispassionately, as is possible only when, concealed and unobserved, one hears of it from another's lips.

"There they were, on every side, strangers waiting for him, like a living wall of his prison. And what could he expect from these people? Pity, perhaps? But that was the one thing he did not need and never had needed. The sympathy which a few good and generous men had sometimes shown him had been to him only a reminder of his misfortune and a measure of his unexampled humiliation. Even to the dead, pity is a burden and an insult. How then can one bear pity while in health and full consciousness? How can a proud man remain alive and look into the eyes of other living men knowing that all he will see is pity?

"Out of what the earth is constituted and contains I had meant to forge an instrument to conquer and control the world; and now it is that world which has made me its instrument.

"Yes, what is Djem Djemshid? A slave, but a slave is more fortunate. As he is led in chains from market to market he may still hope to find a kind master; he can still harbor hope of a ransom, or a chance to escape. But Djem may not look for kindness, nor could he accept it were it offered. Ransom? Vast sums are collected for him but not as ransom money. On the contrary, both sides pay fortunes to assure that he remain a slave and not be ransomed. (The only exception is his mother, that indomitable, wonderful woman, a creature above all creatures, who yet, by her unavailing efforts, only adds to the load of his humiliation.) Escape? It is hard enough for a nameless slave to slip from his chains; but when he does, he has some hope of eluding his pursuers and losing himself in a world of his own where he can live as a free, nameless man among other free, nameless men. But for Djem no such possibilities of escape exist. All the inhabited world, ranged in two camps, Turkish and Christian, contains no place of refuge for him. Whether on this side or that, he can take only one place: that of a Sultan, victorious or defeated, alive or dead. And so he is a slave for whom there can be no escape, not even in thoughts or dreams. Escape is the path and hope of humbler and happier men. But Djem is condemned to be Sultan, whether here in captivity or in his rightful place in Istanbul, or dead and in his tomb. A Sultan and only a Sultan can he be, and only as a Sultan can he find salvation; a

Sultan and nothing less, since for him that would be the same as ceasing to exist as himself and nothing more, since there can be nothing greater. It is a slavery from which there is no escape, even after death.

"The ship gave a muffled sound as its buffers scraped against the stone pier. The silence was such that it could be felt. Like a faint palpitation it passed along the quay where everyone, from cardinal to groom, was motionlessly watching the stately man with the gold-wreathed high white turban on his head, how he stood apart, three or four paces in front of his followers like a statue. There was not one among them who did not see in him a Sultan and who did not sense that Djem could be nothing else, even though it brought him to ruin."

Saying this, Djamil rose to his feet. (In order not to allow the warders to hustle him to his room like the rest, he usually went of his own accord, just before the appointed time.) After his customary gentle farewell he disappeared in one of the windings of Devil's Yard, where the shades of dusk were already poking into the farthest corners.

7

The young man did not appear on the second, nor yet on the third day. About noon Haim came and casting wary, searching glances all round him, said that "something bad had happened" to Djamil. More than this even he had been unable to learn.

Just two days later Haim, who had meanwhile not been idle, turned up with an account of Djamil's disappearance already fitted together.

At first, with dark looks and head held down, he paced around Brother Petar in ever narrowing circles and ellipses, shooting glances around him from under his eyebrows. He was obviously trying to give his conversation the appearance of a chance encounter, not realizing, of course, how futile and transparent his "precautionary measures" were. When he came quite near, he asked in a stifled voice:

"Did they question you yet?"

"No," replied Brother Petar loudly. Haim's "measures" had begun to be a bore. Still, hoping that Haim had found out something about Djamil, he repeated in a friendlier tone:

"No. But what's the news?"

Haim then began his story. At first he sought to give the impression of a man who had halted casually, in passing, and would be moving on immediately, and he kept up his anxious glancing around him; but little by little he forgot himself and he spoke with growing intensity, though without raising his voice.

Here and there his account was unclear and even incomprehensible but the rest was described with such sharp detail that he sounded like an eyewitness. Haim knew everything and had seen what it had been quite impossible to see.

When, at first dusk, Djamil had withdrawn to his cell, which the guard had locked behind him, it was still light in the spacious room. A supper such as was served to none of the other prisoners was already laid and was growing cold in two gleaming, covered dishes. It was all as it had been every evening before: the pacing from end to end of the locked room; the waiting for the sleep which one knows will not come. Down in the Yard the last sounds died away. The dusk darkened the white walls and seemed to tighten them around the sleepless man. In the new nocturnal world that came into being, unreal voices and faint lights rose from the things fitfully seen and heard in the darkness and stillness. Suddenly, he himself could not tell just when, he thought he heard a key searching for, and finding, the keyhole. And this time it was not an auditory illusion. The door did in fact open and a dim light showed in the doorway. Two shadowy men entered the room without a sound. Behind them a servant carried a little oil lamp. He stepped to one side, raised the lamp and remained motionless in that position.

The lamp lighted up the whole scene. One of the two men was stout: everything about him was round and soft; his person, his voice, and his movements. The other was thin, all bone and muscle in a tanned skin, with large eyes sunk in shadows, and huge, fearsome fists which stood out in the light. The couple looked like personifications of the Sultan's ambiguous justice. Only the first man said good evening politely, with a dangerous politeness. Then it began.

In his ominously polite voice the stout official said that the first interrogation had been a formal preliminary and the questions and answers had, of course, merely laid the basis for further inquiry.

"It is necessary that you tell us, Djamil Effendi, for whom you have been collecting facts about Djem Sultan and for whom you have worked out in such detail the way in which a plan of rebellion against the lawful Sultan and Caliph can be put into execution and what ways and means can be found of seizing the throne with the aid of enemies from abroad."

"For whom?" repeated the young man quietly. He was now completely on his guard.

"Yes, for whom?"

"For myself and for no one else. I made a special study of an episode well known in our history. I went deeply. . . ."

"But why, out of all the subjects on which learned books have been written, did you pick on this?"

Silence.

(Haim had by now entirely forgotten his caution and spoke with animated facial mimicry and gesturing hands.)

"Listen," the stout official went on calmly and with exaggerated courtesy—"You are an intelligent, educated man of a distinguished family. You must see for yourself that you have involved yourself in an awkward affair—or someone else has involved you. You know, too, that today, as at that time, there is a Sultan and Caliph on the throne (may God grant him life and all success!) and that a matter like this is an unsuitable subject even for private meditation, not to speak of research, writings and discussion. You know that no word, even when spoken in the depths of the forest, remains unheard, certainly not when it is written or told to others as has been done by you in Smyrna. So explain the matter to us and tell us everything. It will be easier for us and better for you."

"Nothing you say has any connection with me or my thoughts."

In the young man's voice sincerity was emphasized by an undertone of resentment. The official abandoned his attitude of polite affability for a manner which came much more naturally to him.

"Wait a bit. There must be some connection. Everything links up with everything else. You're a learned man, but we're not complete dunces. One doesn't undertake such work casually or without some objective."

Since all the questions were put by the stout man Djamil concentrated his attention on him and on the questions he was asking. And his replies were cautious echoes of the questions.

"Objective? What objective?"

"That's just what we should like to hear from you."

The young man made no reply. Thinking that he was wavering, the stout man added imperatively, prolonging each syllable:

"Now then, if you please!"

This was said in a new tone of voice, harsher and drier, with a hint of impatience and menace.

The young man glanced into the dark corners on either side of him, as if searching for a witness beyond that weak ring of light. He was searching for the revealing word or sentence that would dispel this idiotic misunderstanding, clear up the whole matter and prove that there was no ulterior motive here and that no other account was necessary or possible, least of all at this hour, in this place and in such a fashion. He thought of saying this but remained silent. And now both officials spoke, the thin one joining in with sharp insistent questions and commands of his own.

"Speak!"

"Tell us, it will be better for you and—simpler."

"Now tell us everything. When did you start all this?"

"Now then, what was your aim and whom were you working for?"

They overwhelmed him with such demands and questions. The young man blinked at the light and cast uneasy glances into the dark corners. He was in a difficult position, unable to grasp what they were saying or distinguish one question from another. And he was suddenly aware that the thin man had drawn quite close to him and, in a raised voice was addressing him familiarly.

"Come on, you, come on now, speak up!"

And this was all he could react to. He felt humiliated, thrown off guard, left defenseless. He wanted to say that his fault and his misfortune were not to have an "objective," and to have been brought (or having brought himself) into a situation in which he could be subjected to such questioning and by people of this sort. And he thought he should tell them so, but he remained silent.

So it went on, and it lasted a long time. At some point during the night, in a time immeasurable by ordinary risings and settings of the sun, and outside the bounds of relationships, Djamil acknowledged openly and proudly that he was identical with Djem Sultan, that is to say, with a man who, unfortunate beyond all others, had reached an impasse, a man for whom there was no escape and who neither would nor could yield or disown himself.

"I am he," he repeated, in that quiet but firm voice in which police-court confessions are spoken, and sank back on his stool.

With a sudden involuntary movement the stout man shrank back, startled into silence. But the thin man apparently shared none of his partner's dismay at facing one who had clearly gone out of his mind and had thus placed himself beyond the world and its laws. Too stupid and callous to understand, the thin policeman sought to make the most of the free field left him by his more intelligent colleague. He put fresh questions, hoping to extort a confession from the young man, implicating him in an actual conspiracy in Smyrna.

Sitting exhausted on the stool, Djamil looked like a man in collapse. The thin man danced round him and sent piercing glances into his eyes. He had before him, he thought, a body without will or consciousness with which he could do just as he pleased, and this spurred and encouraged him to still greater arrogance. At one point, it seems, he placed one of his formidable fists on Djamil's shoulder. The young man, incensed and probably disgusted by such insulting familiarity from such a creature, thrust him sharply away. Immediately a fight began in earnest. The other policeman joined in. Djamil defended himself, with a force and agility nobody would have expected of him. In the melee the servant was knocked down together with the lamp he was holding and when he managed to extricate himself from the whirl of fists and feet he ran out and raised the whole guard-house, adding to the noise of the battle going on within the dark cell. It was from this servant and from the prisoners roused by the clamor that the news got round the Yard of the nocturnal scene with the young man from Smyrna; and whatever is whispered round the Yard, Haim gets to know.

That same night they took Djamil out of the Yard through a side door.

Alive or dead? And where had he been taken to?—

was all Brother Petar could think of in his consternation. Haim already had the answers to these questions.

If alive, he had probably been taken to Timarkhan, near the Sulemaniyeh, where mental cases are imprisoned. There, among lunatics, his fantasy of himself as heir to the throne would be like any other madman's notions, harmless fancies of a sick man of which no one takes any notice. In any case, these sick and deranged men do not live long and disappear quickly and easily, together with their delusions, and nobody has to account for it.

On the other hand, if the struggle had been desperate enough, if the youth, grappling with his two assailants, had managed to wound one of them (and it looked as if this had been so, since they afterwards had to clean the room of traces of blood), then the officials might well have gone still further, since blows are by no means rationed here and easily exceed what is strictly necessary. In that event the unfortunate son of Tahir Pasha would already be in his grave, and a grave of the sort whose stone bears no inscription, and tells nothing and certainly nothing about emperors and their disputes and battles with rivals.

When he had spun out his tale to the end, Haim's fears of the "dangers" which surrounded him returned. Without taking leave, casting searching looks about him, he moved on, again trying to give the appearance of a man strolling aimlessly about the spacious Yard.

Brother Petar clenched his teeth feeling a sudden rage at his own fate, and detesting everything around him, even that harmless Haim with his incessant need to ferret out everything and weave his intricately detailed stories and spread them around. And a new thought entered his mind and put him into such a cold sweat, he had to wipe his forehead. Staring distractedly at the gray trampled earth and the white walls before him, as if he were seeing them for the first time, he felt a chill, thin gush of fear through his whole body—fear lest they should start questioning him about his conversations with Djamil. This might well subject him, an innocent man, for a second time to a senseless inquisition. It was true enough that Haim was a nervous fellow and saw dangers where none existed; still, anything might happen.

Hard on this thought pressed another: what could have become of Djamil? At that he was seized again with a sick feeling aggravated by the fact that he could give no active form to the compassion he felt, and made almost unbearable by the uncertainty. Now he felt an urgent need to get away, to see and hear people unrelated to these sinister, labyrinthine tales of Smyrna, to be among people of any sort, provided they were outside that ensnaring maze in which the delusions of the insane and traps set by the police were entangled and in which he had been caught.

He walked down the Yard toward a shaded side where scattered groups of prisoners were noisily quarreling, gaming or joking.

8

Two or three days passed and with them Brother Petar's fears of being interrogated about his long conversations with Djamil. That meant that the whole affair was finished and—buried. His fear and suspense over his own danger were at an end, yet that made it no better or easier for him. On the contrary. Now began the ordeal of the days without Djamil. He could not forget him and he felt there was no hope of his return.

The summer heat was not yet over. In the Yard everything was as it had always been. Some departed, others arrived to take their place, and one did not even notice it. They were all incidental and unimportant. The Yard lives its own life. Through a hundred changes it is always the same.

Every morning the same or similar groups of prisoners gathered in the shade. Brother Petar joined the
nearest group of "neighbors." Everything remained the
same. As ever Zaim was marrying and divorcing imaginary wives and, as ever, coarse and malicious men were
inciting him to further falsehoods, and others enjoyed
the spectacle. Zaim's face had a greenish pallor, as if he
suffered from jaundice. And through all his fabrications
his frightened, roving eyes betrayed his desperate secret
fears of the doom awaiting him if the charges against
him were sustained.

Other men too were talking of women, but not of
wives. Usually the muscular man with the hoarse bass
voice was the loudest. At this moment he has yielded
place to an old sailor describing the young Greek bar-
maid who served at their inn.

"I've never seen a better-stacked female. Forward
she heaves a pair of breasts like the best-stuffed pillows;
and her stern turns behind her like a couple of millstones.
All the men used to reach out for a grab at her wherever
and however they could. She fought them off and the
innkeeper, a gap-toothed Greek, also used to fend them
off. But who's to keep sailors' hands off? They kept pat-
ting and pinching her and in the end she had to leave.
At least, that's what the innkeeper said. But she didn't,
of course. The old fox hid her away in his home and kept
her for himself. The sailors cursed him and groaned. 'Eh,

what a shame, a woman like that! So well-stacked. A real haystack!' 'Haystack' repeats the old sailor as if to himself. "But if things had gone on like that, with everyone plucking they would have pulled the 'haystack' apart, straw by straw, the pigs!"

"Eh," the husky bass started up. "Eh, eh, what a fellow! You can talk of nothing but bar sluts, eh! Nothing but smut, eh!"

An argument started, from which the bass emerged the victor. Everyone shushed the sailor and asked the bass to go on with a story he had begun. And on he went in a confused but exciting tale of a Georgian woman whose beauty had been the sensation of Istanbul and who had died young.

"The whole family's like that. Her grandmother was a famous beauty. The whole of Tiflis was mad about her. Yes, they moved her out of Tiflis to a relative's home in a village. Because of her the village is now called 'Seven Stretchers.' Before that it had another name, I don't know what. Because of her seven men infatuated with her beauty died in half an hour in front of her house in a battle among men who had come to carry her off and men who rushed to protect her. Three families went into mourning, and she herself died of grief. She didn't slowly pine away, she died as if she'd been nipped by the frost. Overnight. But even as she lay dying she wouldn't tell whom she had preferred nor whether he was one of the dead or one of the survivors. Well, from this grandmother she had inherited her beauty, her figure, her eyes. . . ."

"Ah yes," somebody broke in, "it's well known that Georgian women have marvelous eyes."

"What's well known? How, well known? What do you know of such things, you blind worm?"

"Why shouldn't he know?" others protested. "Are you the only man in the world with eyes in his head?"

"Don't interrupt the man. Let him go on with his story."

"Carry on, man; don't let them bother you."

The big man with the big voice angrily waved his hand as if waving off these appeals. With a scowl he said, "Why should I go on? Why should I waste my breath talking to that nitwit?"

But they pressed him to continue and finally, as always, he allowed himself to be calmed down and, though keeping up his show of annoyance, resumed his story of the Georgian beauty and her fabulous eyes.

"When someone says just like that 'she had marvelous eyes,' I see red. Eyes, indeed, blast your own! When you look at those two eyes of hers, you don't so much as think of the two peepers each of us carries in his head, but of two scenes of heaven lighted by sun and moon. What stars and clouds, what miracles there are in those two eyes! You poor fool! You look and you turn to stone and then you melt away. You're finished. Aren't those more than mere 'two eyes'? They see you, of course, but that's the last and least thing about them. Eyes! What are these miserable eyes we carry in our heads, which help us to find the door and not to miss our mouth with the spoon compared to those two heavenly miracles? But there's no comparing them. They're a something that has happened only once on this earth, once and never again. It's just as well. Less trouble and grief. Such eyes shouldn't die like others; or rather they should never have been born into this world."

The man went suddenly silent, as if his voice failed him. And not a word came from the group. But the pause was momentary. The wrangling promptly resumed, the laughter, the curses, the confused babble.

At this point, Brother Petar felt someone at his side. When he turned to go, Haim stood before him.

Brother Petar had become used to such sudden confrontations with Haim. Driven by his fears and suspicions the poor man, laden with a pack of possessions, kept changing his havens, kept flitting from group to group, too uneasy to stay put anywhere. No sooner had he settled somewhere then he began his "precautionary measures," and in a day or two resumed his vain hunt for a safer berth. He would even pass Brother Petar sometimes as if he did not know him; at other times he would greet him only with a slight nod, and a meaningful wink; and at still other times he would stop and talk freely until he suddenly remembered something and moved on.

It was in this way now that he stopped to talk to Brother Petar to tell him about the muscular man with the deep voice. About him, too, Haim had found out everything.

A man of low birth, his great strength and shrewdness had won him a place among the gentry. For some years he had been a champion wrestler, famous all over Turkey. He had been an army contractor, had run a coffeehouse, then acted as agent in deals of all kinds. Fortunes had passed through his hands. He was also a gambler, a heavy drinker and, above all, a wencher, and had contracted a venereal disease. His hands had never been clean and he had never distinguished between "mine" and "thine," but until he succumbed to the disease, he had managed to come through every scrape unharmed. He had fallen ill two or three years back, and since then he had sunk lower and lower and had lost his grip altogether. Women had sapped his brains and his bodily strength was failing. Avoided by his former friends he began to associate with the lowest criminals. This had landed him in the Yard, a bankrupt many times over and a felon. It was barely two months that he had been here under interrogation and he was visibly failing from day to day. The wits that remained to him were dimming and he could no longer distinguish between what was, what might be and what had never been. His talk was fixed on women, and this obsession was a disease in itself. He had become incapable of conceiving of women or of love-making except as participant. He could not bear any mention of it by another. And in this mania he was disintegrating like a lump of sugar in water. To the one-time wrestler and man-about-town nothing was left but this petty wrangling and garrulity. Lately he had grown more irritable and had lost weight. At the same time he had become less uncouth and his tales had taken on a livelier and more feeling quality. His once famous voice had grown hoarse, but it was now more charged with emotion breaking at times into sobs from which he tried to divert attention by abusing people around him.

"That broken barrel can't stop talking now. His hoops are gone and you can see he's leaking all around. He's done for."

In a loud and confident voice, almost cheerfully, Haim went on talking of everything and everyone. Then suddenly he broke off, looked around him like a man who has just awakened, winked both eyes as a secret sign to his uncomprehending companion, and without a word of farewell straggled off with slow steps and head down, a man looking for something he had never lost.

And Brother Petar continued his stroll down the Yard, and approaching some other group, wondered were there anywhere such things to be found as a sane man or sane talk, seeking at least distraction or forgetfulness as a man in pain seeks sedatives.

It has been said before, and it is true, that life in the Yard never changes. But the seasons change and with the seasons some aspects of its life change. It begins to get dark earlier. A shudder is felt at the thought of autumn and winter, of the long nights and the cold, damp days. The life ahead of Brother Petar seemed unvarying, a long, dimly lit corridor; yet day by day one felt it shrinking an inch or two; and this feeling sent spasms of panic through all the prisoners, even the toughest of them.

Brother Petar often recalled those days. Lifting himself from time to time and propping himself up on the pillow, he gazed into the snowy distance, following memory's footprints, and spoke in a low, clear voice:

"I could see my imprisonment dragging on and on, through no fault of my own. So long as I was preoccupied with poor Djamil and his troubles I could forget my own. But now I could no longer evade them. I told myself to be patient, but patience failed me. Long nights, still longer days, and burdensome thoughts. The worst was knowing myself innocent and anxious to prove it. Yet no one questioned me and no message came from outside. Sometimes, when I thought of it, the blood mounted to my head till I couldn't see, and I had to restrain myself from shouting at the top of my voice in pain and rage. Still, I managed to control myself, held on and lived on my own fat, wondering what might still be in store for me. My situation was clear enough but I couldn't see any way out. There was no one to talk to about it and I was dying of idleness and having nothing to occupy me. That was the worst. I'm not used to it. No books, no tools. I asked was there any work for me to do, mending a coffee mill or a clock. Anything, because that's my trade. But the guard wouldn't even answer me. I begged him then to ask his chief. Next day he told me: 'Sit quiet and don't mention it again,' and turned his back on me. I wanted to put myself right with him but he cut me short with an ugly gesture:

" 'Sometimes one of them smuggles in a file or a chisel to help him escape. We certainly don't issue them ourselves. That wasn't such a clever idea of yours!'

"And with these words he spat and went away. I was left standing like a statue. I wanted to call after him that I only wanted something to do, that I had had no thought of escaping. At that moment I could have cried like a baby, I don't know why, and I felt ashamed. But when I had thought it over a bit, I saw that what the man had said was right and the fault was mine more than his. Where had been my wits? When people sink to where I had sunk, no one can trust them. I had forgotten where I was!

"And so once again, idle and anxious, I waited for the passing of day and the coming of night, which passed even more slowly.

"One day they released the two merchants from Bulgaria, and instead of sending them into exile allowed them to go home. According to custom and by way of charity, they gave me the reed mat on which they had been lying. 'Take it,' said one of them, 'and may the sun warm you too'—all this in a whisper and turning his head to one side. They went off like two shadows, not daring even to show their joy. Without them it became still drearier for me. And on top of my own worries I kept thinking of Djamil and his sufferings and his fate. I began to imagine things.

"I used to get up very early, at dawn even, and could not wait for the door to be opened. I would hurry from the stench of confinement and wash myself at the fountain, then sit down and just bask in the light until the crowd came swarming out of their cells. And what a daybreak there is in Istanbul! It's indescribable. I had never seen the like before and never shall again. (As if God had conferred all earth's beauty upon the Evil One.) The sky grows rosy, then spreads over the earth. There's enough for all, for the rich and the poor, for the Sultan and the slave and the prisoner. So I used to sit and enjoy it and smoke, if a smoke could be found, and my head would be whirling with the tobacco. There would be smoke all round me, and beside me would appear, as it were, Djem-Djamil, sleepless, pale, with tears in his eyes. And I would talk to him simply and sincerely, as I had never been able to nor known how while he was here and we used to see each other, just as I would have talked to one of the young friars from my monastery when he had an attack of *taedium vitae*. I would take him by the shoulders and shake him.

" 'I got up early, ahead of the dawn. It's daylight. Hey, Djamil Effendi!'

"But he would shake his head.

" 'For me, it's all one,' he'd say, 'midnight or dawn. There's no daybreak.'

" 'What do you mean, no daybreak, my poor dear brother? Let's not have such silly blasphemy! So long as there's dusk there'll be dawn. Don't you see all this heavenly beauty?'

" 'No, I don't,' he would say with his head down and his voice breaking.

"And grief would come over me and I didn't know what I could do to help him. All round us Devil's Yard was swimming in sunlight.

" 'Come, my poor fellow, don't talk as you shouldn't and lay sin upon your soul. God will grant you recovery from your sickness and you will look again, in health and freedom, on everything that's good and beautiful.'

"He only hung his head.

" 'I can't,' he said, 'my dear man, I can't get well, be-cause I'm not ill. I am as I am, and one can't be cured of oneself.'

"And he would keep up this melancholy talk, con-fusedly and obscurely. It was enough to make the tough-est of us weep. I tried in vain to comfort him. I scolded him as a father scolds a son for ignoring what's before him and seeing what's not there. And to tell the truth, the bright morning turned to darkness, in a way, for me too. Then I'd turn to joking again. I'd take out my to-bacco.

" 'Come, let's have a smoke, and puff off the Evil One.'

" 'Yes,' he would say, but only to humor me.

"He would take a smoke but who can say where his thoughts were. And he smoked, as it were, with dead lips and looked at me through his tears, poor Djem. Soon his cigar would go out.

"Somewhere somebody cried out (two men were fighting) and caught my attention. I looked up and there was nobody at my side. My cigar had gone out in my still upraised hand. I must have been talking to myself! My hallucination gave me a scare. I feared insanity like the plague and I realized that here even the sanest of men sometimes lose their balance and begin to see things.

"I started to fight for my sanity. I forced myself to remember who and what I was, where I came from and how I had got here. I repeated to myself that outside this Yard there was another quite different world, that this place wasn't everything and wasn't forever. And I struggled not to forget that and to hold on to this thought. And I sensed how the Yard could suck a man down to its murky bottom, like a whirlpool."

It's not easy for even the toughest man to last through such a day and wait for nightfall with such thoughts. Day after day brought no change and no hope: only Haim. When he came. He came every day but there could be no real conversation with him. He, poor wretch, sank ever deeper into his gloomy tales and imaginary fears.

In vain Brother Petar kept asking him what he had heard of Djamil. He knew nothing and no longer cared to find out. He seemed not even to remember the young man from Smyrna. He was brimful of other fearful and upsetting tales which he recounted with the same urgency in full detail, as if he himself had seen them and lived through them. Then he would forget them all just as quickly. It seemed as if for him the whole world could not hold enough bad news, injustice or suffering. He recorded them all, transmitted them, then forgot them.

Haim would come, go through his ritual of "measures" and sit beside "the one man you can really trust

131

here," and Brother Petar would put on a forced show of amiability and clap him on the shoulder.

"Well, Haim, my old cure for care, what's the news?"

But Haim would gaze at him with a dark, glazed look in his unevenly set eyes and would say, in a muffled voice, as if he had not heard Brother Petar's words:

"Listen. I don't know whether you've ever thought of it, but lately my mind's turned to it more and more; there's not one soul here who hasn't been driven out of his wits. Believe me. They're all sick and crazy—guards, prisoners and spies (and they're nearly all spies!) not to speak of the biggest lunatic of them all, Karadjos. In any other country on earth he'd have been in an asylum long ago. In short, they're all mad except you and me."

His voice trembled. This made Brother Petar raise his eyes and take a better look at him. Haim had lost weight, he was as unshaven as ever, his eyes were red and watering as if he had been sitting a long time at a smoky hearth. His head just perceptibly shook, and his voice had fallen down to a frightened whisper.

"They're all crazy, on my honor."

A shudder of anxiety went down Brother Petar's spine. For a moment he felt that there was, in truth, no way out of Devil's Yard.

But on that very day he got the first glad news from outside.

He was strolling around the Yard as he did every

morning. Two young prisoners, hardly more than boys, were chasing around using him as the centerpoint of ever narrowing circles. Annoyed, he tried to break away from these exuberant youths when one of them brushed against him and he felt a folded scrap of paper thrust into his hand. The youths continued their chase but now in widening circles, and Brother Petar, puzzled and perturbed, withdrew to an isolated corner to read the note. On the paper, in Turkish, in a hand unknown to him, was written: "Petar will be released in a day or two."

He spent that day and the following night in tremulous speculation. He could draw no other inference than that Brother Tadija was the sender of the note.

And the following day, sure enough, the guard came and told him to collect his belongings and make ready to travel. Early that evening he was led out and sent into exile at Acre. Had he not already been convinced that the note came from Brother Tadija, this would have confirmed it, since Brother Tadija had never, in all his life, foreseen anything accurately.

That night, from the Asian coast, where the exiles were assembled before setting off, Brother Petar saw for the first and last time Istanbul at its most majestic and beautiful. The air was soft and mildly scented. But he felt bewildered and lost among the score of his fellow voyagers. It was a night without stars or moon. And along one horizon, Istanbul rose, like a display of fireworks frozen in flight. The month was Ramadan, and on the minarets of all the mosques candles were twinkling like constellations above the innumerable lights of the city. Most of the exiles sat with bowed heads. Some were already lying down. Brother Petar had once seen Istanbul by day; now, at night, it looked like some mighty exhalation of light, a great wave crested with points of fire, a ring set against the invisible sky and the boundless night. (What did it cost to kindle all those lights? Who would ever be able to put them out?) It seemed to him there could be no place there for the Devil's Yard, and yet there it was, somewhere, in one of those dark spaces between the spangles of lights. Tired, he turned to the other side, towards the dark, silent Eastern horizon; but here too, his thoughts were on the Devil's Yard. It had accompanied him on his journey and was to travel with him, waking and sleeping, to Acre, and to remain with him during his sojourn there, and forever after.

"At Acre, too, I saw and experienced all kinds of things. I've told you something of it and there are still things I could tell. There I met many exiles, of every religion and race, many criminals and many more innocents. Many had also spent months in Devil's Yard and had known Karadjos. One young fellow from Lebanon, an excellent mimic, had caught his walk and his intonations and we roared with laughter when he strutted before us shouting: 'What's that you say? You're not guilty, not to blame? Eh, that's fine, we need one just like you, here!'

"He was a squat man, broader than he was tall, with a big shaven head and spectacles with thick lenses, and he was full of jokes and laughter. He was a Christian. When we got to know each other better and I had told him who I was and where I came from I saw that he was a good deal cleverer and more formidable than he appeared. Some sort of politician, it appeared. Done with his joking he would sit down beside me and say, still laughing, 'Ah, he was good, Karadjos.'

"I would show my astonishment. 'He, good? A wretched kind of goodness!'

" 'No, no. As things are today he was the right man in the right place.' Then in a voice lowered to a whisper he said, in my ear: 'If you want to know what a state and its government are like and what future it has, just try to find out how many honest, innocent men are in jails and how many frauds and criminals are walking around free. That'll give you best measure.'

"This was all spoken offhand, as it were. Then he would suddenly get up, put his hands in his pockets, and strut and bawl like Karadjos and set us all laughing again. But through all this clowning I kept thinking of Djamil and I was sad not to have someone to talk to about him. I don't think I ever felt so sorry for a living creature."

Brother Petar stayed eight months at Acre. Then,

at the intervention of his brethren and of some influential Turks, he was released and returned to Bosnia, at the same time of the year as he had set out, a year earlier, together with Brother Tadia Ostrojic, who had remained in Istanbul all that time and had made every effort to free him.

And so it ends. There is nothing more. Only a grave lost among the others in the graveyard, lost like a white mound among other white mounds in illimitable snow. No more tales or storytelling. As if there were no world left worth the effort of seeing, walking, breathing. No more Istanbul or Devil's Yard. No more young man from Smyrna, who died once before his death when he imagined himself the Sultan's luckless brother Djem. No more wretched Haim. No more black Acre. No more strivings and the struggles, hopes and despairs they give rise to. Nothing. Only snow and the simple fact that men die and are returned to earth.

So it seemed to the young man by the window, who had been, for a moment, carried away by the remembered tales and over whom the thought of death had cast a shadow. But only for a moment. Weakly at first, then more urgently, as if to one waking up, the voices from the next room grew louder, as did the dull clang of metal objects thrown on the pile, and Brother Mijo

Josic's harsh voice dictating the list of effects left by the late Brother Petar.

"Go on. Write: one steel saw, small, German. One."